MW01244458

Dawn Stories:

Tales About Our Paleolithic Ancestors

By
Paul A Trout, Ph D

Illustrated by Kathleen Lynch

Dawn Stories

Dawn Stories by Paul A Trout, Ph D

Copyright © 2018 by Trout Pond Publications. All rights reserved.
PO Box 511, Oak Lawn, IL 60454

No part of this book may be reproduced in any written, electronic, recording, or photocopying without written permission of the publisher or author. The exception would be in the case of brief quotations embodied in the critical articles or reviews and pages where permission is specifically granted by the publisher or author.

To purchase books at a bulk discount, to request a personal appearance reading by the author, or to set up a book signing, visit www.dawnstories.com.

Illustration and Cover Art by Kathleen Lynch – lynchart2000@yahoo.com

Editing & Publication Assistance by Dave Trout at UTR Media – utrmedia.org

Page Editing by Goran and the staff at Book Design Team – bookclaw.com

Author Photography by Kathleen Ugrin

ISBN: 978-1-7322887-0-6
10 9 8 7 6 5 4 3 2 1
1. Fiction 2. Prehistoric 3. Paleolithic
First Edition

Paul A Trout, Ph D

DEDICATION

To my aunt, Ruth Zimmerman, who, when her eyes
failed her, asked me to read these tales to her over the
phone, caring for the People as much as I did.

Table of Contents

Preface

The idea for DAWN STORIES came to me in a dream. The day before, I had been doing research for a non-fiction book about the Paleolithic background to storytelling. The project had been preoccupying me for many months. Then one night my imagination transported me back *into* the Paleolithic. At first, I saw myself observing a group of ape-like early humans as they went about their tasks. But then, I saw myself joining them, becoming one of them, though how ape-like I had become the dream did not make clear. I wanted to explain things to these people, tell them what things were and how things worked. But I could not speak to them, nor they to me. The dream had transported me to time when language had not yet come into existence. Here I was, a writer, who had dreamed himself into a story where there were no words. When I awoke the next morning, I could think only of the people I had met in my dream, about the challenges they faced without language, and about the challenge of writing an account of such people. DAWN STORIES is my attempt to meet that challenge. After a year of living amongst the People, I finally returned to the non-fiction book that got it all started. But the People continue to visit me in my dreams, as if asking me to create more tales about their struggles to survive so very long time ago.

Let the Kentibori storyteller initiate you into this group of early humans struggling to survive in the deep past. Join them as they find a new cave to call home, as Burning Stick and Eyes that Laugh hide from a "bad one" (a cave bear), as Hair on Face is pulled from the mouth of an "old one" (a crocodile), as Eyes that Laugh stares down a lion, as the People steal antelope meat from the jaws of a leopard, as Sign Reader leads the People though the dangerous forest and grasslands of ancient Africa, and, as the slightly crazed Fast Climber invents storytelling. The People have no language, but they communicate with each other and care for each other. They fear what they don't understand, but they are driven to understand what they fear. *Dawn Stories* attempts to depict what life may have been like for our primordial ancestors at the dawn of humanity. It's an adventure story as engrossing as the tales of Sinbad or Jack London's *Call of the Wild*. For at the beginning, every day was an adventure.

Gather Round Me and Hear My Stories of the First People

I am the storyteller of the Kentibori people. I have been their storyteller for many many years. After all this time my hair is now grey, my skin is as rippled as wind-blown desert sands, and my arms and legs are as skinny as the sticks used to fence off the vegetable gardens. My lips have become thin, my nose has become long, and my ears droop as if melons were hanging from them. When I sit on the ground and cross my legs, my shoulders almost rest on my knees.

All these are signs that I will soon join my ancestors. But when this happens, the storytelling will not stop. Another storyteller will take my place, just as I took the place of the storyteller before me, and that storyteller took the place of another, and that one took the place of another, and so on as it has been since the distant days of the first storyteller of the people.

I tell stories about many things. About how things got their names, about how things came into being, and about how people learned to live with each other and with the animals around them. But on certain nights, when I fall deep into the tobacco trance, I am able to journey back to the time of the first people. I see them as if I were there with them, as if I were one of them. At these times I become more like them than myself. During my trance I tell stories about the ancient ones with their eyes, with their bodies, and with their minds.

When I tell these stories, the Kentibori people listen without moving, staring into the flames as if they were watching dancing snakes. I tell story after story about the first people, about how they lived, about how they died, and, about how they became the first people to tell stories, even before they could speak.

Tonight I make you a member of the Kentibori people. Draw near to me, and listen to my frail voice tell stories about our distant ancestors as if I am one of them. As I say to my people within the glow of the fire, "let us abide with the ancients tonight."

1. Hear My Tale of a New Home

Darkness was chasing the light from the sky and the People were looking for a cave for the night. The People had to climb over big rocks and some of the People slipped and fell. Some held out their hands and feet to help the others climb. Cave-Finder climbed the rocks without falling or looking back. His eyes always looked up and his hands and feet always took him where his eyes were looking. Soon the People could not see him but they could hear him. He was shouting *heeheeah*, "come and look."

The People looked up and saw Cave-Finder standing far away and high above their heads. He called again, *heeheeah*. The People called back, *weeeahah*. They kept climbing up the smooth rocks. It was like climbing many tree-homes without resting. The chests of the People went in and out and the feet inside their chests were running. Their mouths were open and dry but their bodies were wet, and the wetness went into their eyes and stung them. One by one the People finally reached Cave-Finder.

He was jumping back and forth from foot to foot. His lips were pulled back and his teeth were tight together. He was making the sound for good, *ehe, ehe*. When the last of the People finally climbed to the mouth of the cave, Cave-Finder motioned for them to follow him inside. They followed to find out what made him happy. What they found inside made them happy too.

The cave was not black inside like the other caves. High above the heads of the People there was a hole that let in the brightness of the hot circle and the blue of the sky. The sides of the cave were wet and smooth, and deep inside the cave was a circle of water the same color as the blue sky. The People found no bones in the cave to make them afraid of Bad Ones. There was no sign of the black things that hang with their heads towards the ground. The People made circles around Cave-Finder and patted him on his head and back because he had done well to find this cave. Now this was the cave of the People.

They hugged and touched their faces together and jumped from one foot to the other as Cave-Finder had done. But then Night-Watcher stopped jumping from one leg to the other and bent over. He looked up at the People but made no sound. His eyes had pain in them and asked questions. Suddenly Night-Watcher's legs wanted to rest and he fell to the ground. His hands tried to pull out the hair on his chest and dig inside to where the footsteps were running wildly. The footsteps inside him were running so hard that some of the People could hear them.

They could hear the feet run then stop, and then run again and then stop again. Night-Watcher was trying to grab the feet inside his chest but his hands could not tear through his skin. Then Night-Watcher bent over and his head touched the ground. His hands stopped grabbing and dropped to the ground. Night-Watcher did not move. The People made sounds in Night-Watcher's ears but the ears did not move either. The People touched Night-Watcher but he did not touch back. The People backed away and looked at Night-Watcher until their eyes burned.

The People left Night-Watcher with his head and hands resting on the ground. They went outside the cave to wait for the circle in the sky to come back from its hiding place. When it had returned, Night-Watcher still had not moved and the People understood that he was not going to move again. It was hard for the People to see behind their eyes a person not moving. People did not move after the Bad Ones had taken them into the grasses to eat them, but People did not stop moving when they were happy and safe from being eaten.

The People tried to see behind their eyes what to do with Night-Watcher. A few made signs that Night-Watcher should be shared as food, but others shook their heads and made the sound *eevooorr* to say that People must not eat People. Finally, First-to-Shout, Far-Cloud, Eyes-that-Laugh and Strong-Branches went to where Night-Watcher was bending over and picked him up and carried him out of the cave to where the high ground stopped. Then they rolled his body down the rocks. Now Night-Watcher would be eaten by the Bad Ones and not by the People. The People were happy that Night-Watcher would not scream when he was being eaten.

The People came together inside the cave and looked for things to eat. They grabbed things with long ears that ran on the ground. They threw these things against the walls of the cave and then pulled them apart. The things with long ears tasted better than Night-Watcher.

2. Hear My Tale about the Big One

Burning-Stick and Eyes-that-Laugh sniffed the air and picked up the scent. The hair on their bodies bushed out with fear. It was the Big One that could walk like the People. It was near. Burning-Stick and Eyes-that-Laugh looked up and saw a narrow blackness in the rocks just above them. They dropped the food they had dug from the ground and scampered to the hold in the rocks and forced themselves inside. He pressed against her, she pressed against him, and they both pressed against the hardness of the rocks. They felt the coldness of the rocks through the hair on their backs. She wanted to make water but the sound and smell would tell the Bad One that People were hiding inside the darkness, and the Bad One would not want to leave until it ate them.

If Eyes-that-Laugh and Burning-Stick made no sound they might not go inside the Big One. The Big One made sounds through wet holes on its face and through its mouth. The sounds were like rocks moving in water. Suddenly, into the darkness came a hand with long hair and sharp curved bones. It did not scratch the ground but waved in the air as the People do when they find each other or when they cannot see in the darkness. The head of the Big One was too big to go inside the hole where Burning-Stick and Eyes-that-Laugh were hiding. The hand of the Big One moved around but its sharp bones did not touch anything soft and went back outside.

The nose of the Big One smelled all the things that had ever hidden in this hole, but it could not smell Eyes-that-Laugh and Burning-Stick. When they could not smell the Big One, they made water inside the cave, and their bodies stopped shaking. They looked in each other's eyes but made no sound. Behind their eyes they saw the other People. Had they smelled the Big One too? Had they hooted or howled warnings? Had they hid inside the darkness or in the tree-homes where the Big One could not follow them?

Then Burning-Stick and Eyes-that-Laugh heard screams they had heard many times before, screams made by the People when being eaten. They listened until the screams stopped. All they heard now were the thunder sounds from the throat of the Big One and the breaking of sticks. Now there were not be as many People.

Burning- Stick and Eyes-that-Laugh crawled out of the hole in the rock as the others slowly came out of their dark places or down from high places. What they saw was the Big One dragging Antler-Bones into the swaying grasses to eat him. On the ground the red water from Antler-Bones now made mud.

The People did not touch the mud but made a circle around it. Some of them waved their arms and made pant sounds, some howled, fell to the ground and rolled in the dirt. Some pulled at their hair and snarled. One of them beat her head with her hands and made water from her eyes. All of them made the sound *hooasa*. Their noises and howls and shouts made even the wind-born sky-dwellers spring into the air from their hiding places in the tree-homes.

These sounds stopped and the People began to kiss and hug and jump until they finally slumped to the ground. The People were happy that only Antler-Bones had been eaten. The People were less, but there was still the People.

3. Hear My Tale about the Nighttime

The hot circle of light was going to the place where it hid from the Bad Ones. It was at night that the Bad Ones most liked to eat, when many eyes could be seen in the darkness, and when the hair of the People moved and stood up. This was the time for the People to hide themselves too.

Some of the People crawled into the rocks while others climbed into the tree-homes. In the tree-homes the People made sounds that took out of their ears the growls and screams coming up from the darkness. These had no meaning but still made the People felt happy because there were so many sounds being made.

Black-Cloud sounded her name over and over again as long as there was darkness but she made the sound softly so as not to wake those who had closed their eyes. Never-See-Me made the sound of her name so that all the People knew where she was hiding. Far-Cloud and Blowing-Ground made their name sounds too but they made them in time with the slow and light footsteps inside their chests. These sounds at night made the People feel strong and safe during the darkness.

Even with all the sounds, the Bad Ones still came at People from the darkness inside their heads. In this darkness the People saw themselves trying to keep from being eaten. They hid, they stood still, they fell to the ground and covered their eyes, or they ran away to a tree-home or cave. These were the things to do, because when the light came back, the People were still safe in their hiding places.

But not always. Sometimes at night the chase inside a person's head would make trouble when the person would try to run as if on the ground. This would make People fall from the tree-home and on to the ground where the Bad Ones waited. The People did not understand why the Bad Ones came to them at night behind their closed eyes but they knew that they did.

The People made the darkness go away with logs that made light. The People used the sound *nakall* for it most of the time. *Nakall* meant friend who does good things. It made the Bad Ones hide from the People and it made meat taste good. When *nakall* lived with them, the people would not become lost to each other in the darkness. They would gather and sit staring at the changing colors of the moving light until the darkness was inside their heads. But it was not easy to embrace this friend or keep it among the People. *Nakall* often left them and went elsewhere. Then the People would have to find where it had gone and go to it and bring it back so it could do its many good things for them.

Burning-Stick had found the hot light many times but the last time was long ago. The people now lived without this friend but did not want to. Without it there was more darkness than they wanted. And too much red water in the meat.

4. Hear My Tale about Drinking at the River

The People were thirsty but could find no water that was waiting for them. The water must have gone elsewhere during the night when the People could not see. When the light time came the People looked at each other and decided they had to go to where the water is always moving. But this was where the Bad Ones drink. The People made the sound *eevooorr* and tried to click their teeth but their mouths were dry to make the sound. Water was more *nakall* than burning logs.

The People made their way through grass higher than their heads. They often stopped to sniff the air and to point their ears towards sounds that made their hair move. Slowly, slowly, the People drew closer to the moving water. Those holding the little ones huddled together as if hiding in rocks. Around them were the ones who grabbed sticks and branches when the Bad Ones came. The People crouched in fear, listened, looked, and sniffed the air in fear, and smelled of fear.

But there was another smell in their noses, and it was the smell of water. This smell made their mouths dry as dirt. Suddenly Hair-on-Face hooted low and broke from the others and ran to the moving water. He threw himself down where the water made mud. He fell on his knees and hands and raised his head to look around but his thirst kept him from seeing.

Hair-on-Face used one hand to push the water into his mouth and the other hand to push away the ground so he would not fall into the water. He did not see or hear the Old One moving towards him under the water, and he did not have time to jump back. The Old One sprang from out of the water faster than grass-eaters jump over it. The only sound was the water jumping into the air and the scream of Hair-on-Face when the Old One bit down on his arm and started to slide back into the moving water with him.

Hair-on-Face pressed his feet into the mud and pushed against the Old One. He yelled and squealed to the People for help. The People heard the sounds and ran with their feet beating the ground as if they were being chased by a Bad One. Burning-Stick, Eyes-that-Laugh, Fast-Climber, Good-Hider, Water-Fall, First-to-Shout all reached for Hair-on-Face. They grabbed parts of him with the grip they use when climbing tree-homes. As they pulled and pulled they also filled the air with screeches and screams.

Then Good-Hider grabbed a big stick, stepped into the moving water, and stuck the stick into the eye of the Old One. When the Old One opened its mouth and lunged toward eat Good-Hider, the People pulled Hair-on-Face back onto dry land while Good-Hider jumped into the bushes. Old One looked at the People with his one eye, and then he slid under the water with the arm of Hair-on-Face dangling from his mouth.

Hair-on-Face had some arm left, but it was spitting dark red water on the ground and on the People who helped him. It would spit, stop spitting, spit again, and then stop again. Water-Fall gripped what was left of the arm with both hands like when she grabbed a stick to hit food as it runs through the grass. Then the others used mud and leaves to cover the ragged hole spitting out the red water. The red water soon stopped. Hair-on-Face curled up his lips and pressed together his teeth and moaned in pain. But he also beat the ground with his feet and turned in circles because he was happy not to be inside the Old One with many teeth. The People were happy too that they had saved Hair-on-Face from beaten eaten. The Old One always eats what it wants to eat, until now.

5. Hear My Tale about Food and Fear

Like the Bad Ones, the People were always looking for something to eat. They all looked together because many eyes and ears and noses found food quickly, and found the Bad Ones quickly too. It was good to find food, but it was better to find the Bad Ones. Finding food was finding fear.

One day all the People left the dark hiding places and tree-homes to search for something to eat. Behind their eyes they could see the place where they had found the soft food that makes their lips push out in a kiss face. First-to-Shout made the *weeeahah* sound that meant "let's go to that place."

Together they moved slowly across the open spaces turning their heads in every direction and even looking up at the sky where Bad Ones came down without a sound to take away one of the People. The People were afraid when there were no tree-homes to hide in.

As the feet of the People's thumped on the ground, small things ran back and forth in fear, and Far-Cloud, Good-Hider, Fast-Climber and Tall-as-Grass grabbed at them. Suddenly Hair-on-Face jumped forward and stepped on one. He lifted his foot with the small thing still in it, and then tore it into pieces, handing the pieces to the nearest People. There was not much to put in their mouths but the People felt good as they chewed. Hair-on-Face pressed the head in his hands until it broke open and he could eat the meat inside. Food that hid in holes in the ground was better than the food the People pulled from the ground. They ate this food only when their stomachs made noises and gave pain. Meat was always good but meat was better when it was put into red logs. Someday Burning-Stick would find such logs again.

As they chased the things that ran on the ground, the People did not see behind their eyes the hanging food any more. They could only see more meat. They lowered their bodies, put their hands together under their knees, and waited for the little things to come out of their holes. They waited and waited. They were still waiting when the wind brought to their noses the scent of Bad Ones. Now the People began to shake. The People sniffed the air to find out where the Bad Ones were, how close they were, and how many there were. Their hair stood up, and their legs wanted to run about like the small things they were killing with their feet.

Then there was a bellow, a squeal, and a roar as when the sky darkens with clouds. This time the Bad Ones found something else to eat, something big, and did not want to eat the People. This made the People came closer together and touch each other, and some made water. The sounds were a sign not only that the People would not be eaten but that there would be meat for them to eat.

The People waited for signs before moving towards the food left by the Bad Ones. They waited until their ears no longer heard roars and the sounds of sticks when stepped on. They waited until the sky-dwellers that show the People where to find meat were not as many. Slowly the People made their way through the tall grass always sniffing the wind, always listening, always looking. The little ones who had to be carried were soothed with whispered sounds and soft strokes.

The People sensed they were near the meat when their ears caught the eating noises of the sky creatures with flapping shoulders. They would leave nothing for the People. Fast-Climber jumped from the tall grass and ran a few steps towards them with his legs kicking and arms waving and his mouth making noises. The meat eaters jumped backwards or up into the sky. They did not take any of the People with them this time.

Then Blowing-Ground ran towards the bones and the other things lying on the red dirt. He moved as fast as falling water. He filled his hands and mouth with the scraps he could pull free from the bones and ran back to those hiding in the tall grass. They grinned and hooted as he placed meat into their waving hands. Eyes-that-Laugh was watching and sniffing for any signs of the Bad Ones. It was not easy to see them in the tall grasses because the Bad Ones were the color of grass. Some might be hiding there and want more to eat.

Eyes-that-Laugh looked at how far away the bones were and how far away the People were. She sniffed the air and looked into the far grasses and did not move her eyes. Suddenly she ran to get more meat. As she reached the bones a Bad One lifted up from the grass. Eyes-that-Laugh stopped. She made no sound or gesture to the People. Her hair moved but her eyes could not. The Bad One had long hair around its face. He looked at Eyes-that-Laugh, and she looked back at the Bad One. Round brown eyes stared into narrow yellow yes.

The Bad One lifted its head and slowly opened its mouth as wide as it could open. The People could see its teeth and its long tongue and even the hole inside its mouth. It then closed its eyes and slowly turned its head and body to walk into the tall grasses where it could not be seen. Eyes-that-Laugh pulled at the strings of meat still left on the bones and stuffed them in her hands and mouth and hung them around her neck. She then moved slowly backwards towards the People huddled in the grass.

This time the People did not grab at the meat. They let Eyes-that-Laugh give it to them slowly. As she did, they touched her with long, light strokes. Eyes-that-Laugh used her eyes to make a Bad One hide itself in the tall grasses. Her eyes did more than laugh.

After the People ate the meat, they saw again behind their eyes the trees with hanging food. When someone made the sound *weeeahah,* the People pushed their way out of the tall grasses and trod across the open ground towards where food was waiting to be picked and eaten. The People were happy that the Bad Ones had not picked and eaten any of them. They kept touching Eyes-that-Laugh along the way.

6. Hear My Tale about Finding Flames

Even the People in the dark holes could smell the smoke on the morning breeze. Those high up in the tree-homes looked to where the land ended and to where a dark cloud slowly went up to the sky. Now the People were happy. They had waited a long time to have again the moving flames that made meat taste good and made the Bad Ones stay away and made the People warm at night. The flames were a friend to the People but they were a friend that did not want to be touched.

The People soon gathered inside the deep cave. They gave off their scents and made gestures and sounds and hugged each other as they stared into each other's eyes. Their faces asked questions and showed fear because sometimes the People who went to find the flames did not come back. Did the flames eat them or did the Bad Ones eat them? Whatever happened to them they did not come back.

The People moved around and between each other, touching and murmuring and gazing. Slowly their bodies formed a circle around Burning-Stick. They murmured the sound of his name again and again—"he who brings back the burning stick." But Burning-Stick did not want to look for the flames alone. He looked at those in the circle and put his hands on Fast-Climber and Far-Cloud. The three of them pulled themselves closer together and sniffed each other's hair. They did not smell fear. Then they put their lips on each other's faces and made smacking noises. Behind their eyes they could see what was to come. They saw themselves walking a long way. They saw the People stroking and patting them when they returned with the friend who did not like to be touched.

The three picked up sticks as thick as their legs to take with them and to bring back when the sticks made colors and clouds and did not want to be touched. On their walk to the heat in the forest the People would use the sticks to kill food and make the soft things fall from branches. Fast-Climber and Far-Cloud and Burning-Stick also carried with them the white skull of the Bad One who walks like the People and smells like the meat found inside a dark cave. The skull was filled with water to drink as they walked. They carried the skull in their arms as if they were feeding a new one.

The People clicked their teeth and made a wail as Burning-Stick, Far-Cloud and Fast-Climber walked away towards the dark cloud rising to the sky. The three kept the sounds of the People in their ears even as the others became smaller and smaller.

Soon the three entered the tall grasses where the Bad Ones lived. They sniffed the air again and again for signs but their noses found only the smell of burning tree-homes. They walked until the light-giver began to hide itself in the ground. This was a sign that the Bad Ones were coming again. The Bad Ones could see in the dark but the People could not, so Burning-Stick, Fast-Climber and Far-Cloud found a tall tree-home to stay in until the light returned. They left their thick sticks on the ground but took the skull of water up into the tree-home with them.

Each took turns climbing up and then waiting to be handed the skull. Once high in the tree-home they placed the water skull where thick branches came together. They then found places where they could rest during the darkness. They did not have to make pictures behind their eyes to do this.

Once again their noses opened their eyes. The smell of the hot wind was strong because it was walking towards them to meet them as a friend meets a friend. This made them feel joy and they shook the branches, but when they shook the branches, the skull filled with water fell to the ground. The three of them looked at each other with narrowed eyes and curled lips. To be without water was not good. Without water people often hit and bit each other and made strange noises with their mouths. It was not good.

The People climbed down the tree-home and picked up the sticks and the empty skull. They tried to smell water but all they could smell was the hot wind that their legs could now feel. Then they heard the sounds made by the little people with tails that also live in the tree-homes. Soon they could see them jumping from branch to branch as they screeched in fear. They were running from the hot wind and from a Bad One in the sky that does not make a sound when it looks for food.

One of the little people fell to the ground at the feet of Burning-Stick, Fast-Climber and Far-Cloud. In an instant they began beating it with their sticks until it did not move. Then they tore it apart and licked its red water. This red water would do for now. Then they picked up the large skull and made their way towards their friend.

The growing hotness of the air and the sound of sticks breaking were signs that they were near the flames. Soon they saw the burning grass and the smoking tree-homes spread out before them. The flames were coming to greet them, but this friend could not be hugged or touched. As the flames got closer, the hair on the People began to curl and smell and their feet were being bitten by the ground.

The People moved away from the red and yellow flames and put their sticks where the flames had made the ground logs black and white. Soon their sticks were red and yellow and making the air grey. Burning-Stick, Fast-Climber, and Far-Cloud jumped up and down and waved the flaming logs. But Burning-Stick felt fear. He had a picture behind his eyes of the sticks falling to the ground as the skull had. Another picture made Burning-Stick suddenly fall to his knees and scoop glowing dirt into the dry skull. The skull would hold their friend and the friend could be fed with little sticks as they returned to the People. A skull filled with heat made Burning-Stick happier than a skull filled with water.

Because the friend had come to meet them, they were not far from the cave. Soon they would be home again, and the People would give Burning-Stick, Far-Cloud, and Fast-Climber as much water as they wanted when they saw the new way their friend had been brought back to them.

7. Hear My Tale about Bones

The People lived among bones, big bones and small, long bones and short, curved bones and straight. Bones were on the ground and in the caves, and sometimes even in the water. Sometimes the bones were piled together and sometimes scattered over the ground. But they were always the color of an eye once the meat had been taken off them.

Bones were made by the Bad Ones. Sometimes the People saw the Bad Ones making these bones. They watched as Bad Ones chased grass-eaters, caught them, bit into their necks and legs, ate them, and make them into bones. Not even the long and sharp bones on the head of the grass-eaters could stop the Bad Ones from making bones. Sometimes the People even found the bones of the Bad Ones. The heads of the Bad Ones did not have long sticks on them, but they did have many teeth. When the People found the skull of a Bad One they would look at it for a long time without moving or making a sound. Behind their eyes they could see the teeth eating them, and then their own bones among the bones lying on the ground.. The People did not like to touch the bones of the Bad Ones.

One day Hair-on-Face was making sure a Bad One was not hiding in a cave the People wanted to enter for the night. He stood where the darkness of the cave started and he sniffed the air. He smelled the strange black things that hung from the top of caves by their feet and an old scent left by the Bad One that could climb tree-homes, but nothing that made him afraid. Hair-on-Face moved into the darkness and took with him a burning stick to see inside the cave. The People sat down and waited where the darkness of the cave began, picking crawling things from each other's hair and eating them. Eyes-that-Water could not see such small things, and had to have them placed on her lips. When the small things tried to crawl away, she would push them back into her mouth and press them with her tongue. Crawling things tasted good to the People.

All of a sudden Hair-on-Face began to grunt and shout from inside the cave, and. The People could also hear his pounding feet as he ran out of the cave with his hair standing straight out. He no longer had the burning log. He made sounds and pointed and turned his body one way and another. He gave a warning sound but also a "come look" sound—*heeheeah*. He was not being chased by a Bad One but his knees trembled and his chest moved in fear anyway.

The people looked at each other to find out what to do. Hair-on-Face stepped back and forth towards the darkness of the cave but kept his eyes on the People. His right arm made the come-with-me gesture. Tall-as-Grass and Water-Fall stepped towards the darkness of the cave. Good-Hider followed but picked up two burning logs to light the way. The four of them were slowly eaten by the darkness of the cave. The rest of the People came together to touch and hug and make sounds and smell each other. As the waited, they burned more logs.

The darkness chased the sky circle into its hiding place in the ground. Now it was as hard to see outside the cave as to see inside the cave. The only light came from the moving flames of burning logs. Then the People could see dark shapes moving on the walls of the cave. Hair-on-Face, Tall-as-Grass, Water-Fall, and Good-Hider were coming out of the darkness into the light of the burning logs. They sat on the ground, looking into each other's eyes without making a sound until Hair-on-Face said *ishsee* gain and again.

Without looking at anyone, He spread his hands as far apart as he could and then opened his mouth and pointed to his teeth. Tall-as-Grass spread his hands from above his head to below his knees. The others who had come out of the cave uttered the sound for skull—*aanaa*. As they said this, the four of them moved away from each other but touching hands to make a shape. Then they looked towards the People who were standing with their mouths open.

Hair-on-Face had found the skull of a Bad One bigger than any skull the People had ever found inside or outside a cave. This Bad One was big enough to eat all the People in one bite. It was big enough to make bones of the other Bad Ones living in the grasses, in the tree-homes and in the caves. The People saw behind their eyes the skull coming to life and taking all the people into its jaws. The People shuddered and then touched and hugged and whimpered. They sensed with a shiver that they must always look for signs of these new Bad Ones if they were not to become bones themselves.

8. Hear My Tale about a Bad One in a Tree-Home

When the darkness came some of the People crawled deep into caves and some climbed into tree-homes. But the Bad Ones could smell People in the caves, and not even burning logs could always keep the Bad Ones from coming inside. The Bad Ones could also smell People hiding in the tree-homes but most of them could not climb up high enough to get to the People. Except for one.

This Bad One had no legs and no arms and no teeth, and it did not growl or roar or make a sound. When it was in the tree-home it looked like a branch, and it moved slowly the sky circle moved. But when it found something to eat it grabbed the food in its mouth and made circles around it until the food stopped moving.

One night a shriek came from one of the People in one of the tree-homes. All eyes opened up. The People understood at once that a Bad One was finding something to eat among the People. The ears of the People heard nothing but the shrieks of the person being eaten, so the People saw behind their eyes a Bad One with no legs and no arms eating one of the People.

The People heard the thud of a large tree branch falling to the ground and looked down. By the light made by the cold circle in the dark sky, the People saw it was Fast-Water who was shrieking. Fast-Water was in the grip of the Bad One with no legs. The Bad One was hugging Fast-Water with its long body and making circles around her. All that the People could see of Fast-Water was her head and one of her arms pushing on the Bad One.

Burning-Stick, Sign-Reader, and Night-Sky-Mover climbed down the home-tree to keep the Bad One from eating Fast-Water. Hooting and grunting they tried to pull apart the circles made by the Bad One's body, but their hands got caught in the circles until they pulled them free. Fast-Water made no sound but looked at them with wide eyes that said nothing. Then the Bad One turned its head towards the head of Fast-Water, opened its mouth as wide as the mouth of the Old One that lives in the moving water, and slowly began to put Fast-Water inside.

Burning-Stick, Sign-Reader, and Night-Sky-Mover grabbed the legs of Fast-Water and pulled and pulled. Their hands took out the hair on Fast-Water's legs, and their feet dug holes in the soft ground but no matter how hard they pulled, there was less and less of Fast-Water to see as she entered the Bad One little by little. Burning-Stick let go of Fast-Water's leg and picked up a log and threw it at the head of the Bad One. The Bad One closed its eyes but did not stop eating Fast-Water. Soon there was nothing to see of Fast-Water, not even red water or bones.

Burning-Stick, Sign-Reader, and Night-Sky-Mover looked at each other and wailed. The People in the darkness of the caves knew what this sound meant. Then Burning-Stick, Sign-Reader, and Night-Sky-Mover climbed slowly back up into their tree-home, looking at every branch.

When the bright sky circle came out from its hiding place in the ground, the People saw that the Bad One had not moved. It was not afraid of the People. It was not afraid of logs thrown at its head. The People could see that this Bad One was as long and as thick as a fallen tree-home. Inside of it they could also could see the shape of Fast-Water.

9. Her My Tale about the Moon

The white light in the night sky was a friend to the People because it let them see the Bad Ones. When the darkness came the People looked up to find the white circle, and were happy when it was over their heads. But sometimes there was no white circle in the sky, or only part of it was there. Still, even a little light in the sky at night made the People happy.

When the white light in the night sky was all there, some of the People could not close their eyes, but move back and forth in the cave or stand up in the tree-homes and move from branch to branch. This is what Night-Sky-Mover did. When the circle was in the night sky, she would jump from one leg to the other, and sometimes raise her face to the light and make the same noise made by the Bad Ones with yellow eyes. When she jumped while inside the cave, Night-Sky-Mover often stepped on those lying on the ground, and her howls made the People in the tree-homes open their eyes in fear. Night-Sky-Mover did not jump and howl every night but only when a circle was in the sky. The People were not happy when Night-Sky-Mover did this.

One night the cold circle of light made Night-Sky-Mover jump and howl more than ever. She even put her feet in the burning logs as she turned in circles at the mouth of the cave. The logs rolled one place and another. The People opened their eyes and squealed in fear and hugged each other for comfort. Then they saw it was Night-Sky-Mover making the noise. The People in the cave made the *huh* face. What should they do? Night-Sky-Mover did not hurt them like a Bad One might hurt them but she made them afraid and unhappy. The noises she made would bring the Bad Ones to the cave to see what food made these sounds.

Sign-Reader and No-Hair saw Night-Sky-Mover jumping on the ground outside the cave and looking up at the white circle in the sky. They looked at each other and then went to Night-Sky-Mover made a circle around her with their arms and pushed against her from the front and back. They held her tighter and tighter. Soon Night-Sky-Mover could not move. But she stilled howled as she looked up at the light in the night sky.

Holding tight Sign-Reader and No-Hair made the sound *shooooo, shooooo* again and again into the ears of Night-Sky-Mover. She heard the sounds and slowly stopped howling. Soon she was making the same sound to them, *shooooo, shooooo*. They stood still and the People saw their bodies by the light in the night sky and heard the sound they made. Then the People too made the sound *shooooo, shooooo* and they felt happy and safe again.

Each time the circle was in the night sky, Night-Sky-Mover would jump and howl, and each time she jumped and howled, some of the People would hug her and make soft sounds in her ears until she became one of the People again.

10. Hear My Tale of Another

The People did not stay in one place for long. They were always looking for food hanging from branches or food they could grab with their hands or step on with their feet or pull from the ground or find sticking to bones. And they were always looking for places with trees-homes and caves and water. They were not looking for other People because there were no other People to look for. Still, the People found one anyway.

One day the People were walking among many tree-homes. They did not walk fast because they had to look at each branch to see if was a Bad One who makes circles around the People and eats them, and they often stopped to sniff the air for signs of other Bad Ones too.

One time the air did not bring the smell of Bad Ones but of something else. Something that smelled like the People but was not the People. The People looked at one another and walked among each other as they touched and sniffed each other. The People were all there. They smelled the scent again but behind their eyes they could not see anything that smelled like the People but was not the People.

As they sniffed the air over and over again, they suddenly turned their eyes to where the tree-homes made the darkness green during the day. They stood still and looked into the green darkness, and pointed their ears there too. No one made a sound, not even the little one who was gripping the hair of Sign-Reader. As they stood still many little red things crawled up their legs and bit them but the People did not slap them but stood without moving as Eyes-that-Laugh had done when she looked into the eyes of the Bad One near the bones with meat.

Then their ears heard coming from the darkness a small branch breaking free of its tree-home. The sound brought with it the same smell of something like the People but not the People. They stood as still as the tree-homes as they felt the heat of the circle in the sky slowly move over their bodies. Their eyes looked into the darkness for a sign to go with the smell and sound. Then Sign-Reader's head jerked forward towards the darkness. The People looked to Sign-Reader and then to where her eyes and ears were pointed.

Something was in the darkness. It was a shape that did not move. The People could not tell if the shape was looking back at them like the Bad Ones look at them. The only sound was made by the sky-dwellers that hide in the tree-homes. The People did not move and the shape did not move. But the bright circle in the sky moved. Suddenly its light made the darkness where the shape was hiding go away. The Peoplesucked in air at the same time. They saw that the shape had become a person. It had the eyes of a person and its eyes were looking at the People. The light from the circle in the sky made the person fall backwards into the darkness of the tree-homes, and the People heard branches being stepped on. The People made the *huh* face.

First-to-Shout took running steps towards the darkness but the People made the sound *oooah* and he stopped and came back to where the others were standing and shivering with the coldness inside their bodies. Who made this person? Did this person live with others? Why did this person look like the People? Why was this person looking at the People as they walked? The People now wanted to sit around the burning logs to become warm again and hold and groom each other, and to see behind their eyes the People-shape that was looking at them from the darkness.

The People would have to watch for this shape as they watched for Bad Ones, because this too could be a Bad One.

11. Hear My Tale of a Sore Foot

Tall-as-Grass had stepped on sticks that bite and bring red spots and make a person squeal. His foot was big with pain and he often sat with it near the burning logs because the heat made the pain go away. But when he walked again, his foot left red spots along the ground. The foot of Tall-as-Grass was now bigger than even the foot of the Big One who walks like the People.

One day the People were looking for food, and had to cross open ground to find it. They did not like open ground because the Bad Ones who came down from the sky could see them. The People looked upwards all the time. They walked slowly so that Tall-as-Grass with his big foot would not be lost.

The People did not smell or hear the Bad Ones hiding in the grass at the edge of the open ground. But the Bad Ones heard and smelled the People. The Bad Ones came out of the grass as fast as the Old One came out of the water to bite into grass-eaters drinking from the river. The People were still looking up at the sky when their ears heard the feet of the Bad Ones pounding the ground. This sound was enough to make them scream and shriek and run towards the nearest tree-homes.

Noise-Maker was pushed to the ground by a Bad One without hair around its face. Noise-Maker did not make a sound as the Bad One bit into her head. Red water spit from the holes and covered the face of the Bad One. The People were climbing up the tree-homes as fast as their hands and feet could move. The Bad Ones jumped up to eat them but the People were out of reach. The People shrieked as they looked at each other and then at the Bad Ones jumping up below them and trying to climb the tree-homes too.

Then the People looked out at the open ground where Noise-Maker was covered by Bad Ones. But there they also saw Tall-as-Grass lying in the dirt with his hands covering his eyes. He had not yet been eaten. The People did not look at the Bad Ones but looked at Tall-as-Grass lying face down on the ground. His foot did not run. All he could do was to fall tdo the ground and hide his face.

The People watched as a Bad One with much hair around its face walked to Tall-as-Grass and sniffed him. Then the Bad One put two feet on the back of Tall-as-Grass and looked down at him. Tall-as-Grass did not move. The sharp bones on the feet of the Bad One made little holes in the back of Tall-as-Grass but Tall-as-Grass did not move. The Bad One leaned down and sniffed the head of Tall-as-Grass. Its long hair rubbed on the back of Tall-as-Grass and made him want to click his teeth and grin but he did not move.

Then the Bad One stepped back and walked to the feet of Tall-as-Grass and sniffed his big foot. It rubbed its tongue over the foot many times. Again Tall-as-Grass wanted to click his teeth and grin but he did not move. Then the Bad One picked up the foot in its mouth but it did not bite down on it to eat it, but let it drop from its mouth. The foot now was covered in the mouth-water of the Bad One. The Bad One backed up and then turned away from Tall-as-Grass and went to the others still trying to eat the People gripping the branches of the tree-homes. Tall-as-Grass did not move from the ground or take his hands away from his eyes.

The People could see that the Bad Ones were not eating Tall-as-Grass but they could not see that Tall-as-Grass was being eaten by the little black crawling all over him. These things crawled into his ears, they crawled into his nose, and they crawled into his mouth. But Tall-as-Grass did not move. It was better to be eaten slowly by these little ones than to be eaten at once by the ones with big teeth.

When the Bad Ones could not reach the People in the tree-homes, they soon went back into the grass, without taking the bones of Noise-Maker. The People made the sound *aya* to tell Tall-as-Grass that the Bad Ones were gone. He jumped up and slapped at the little ones crawling through the hair on his body. The ones on his face he pushed into his mouth and clicked his teeth from the good taste. The People in the tree-homes drew back their lips and made short hoots when they saw that Tall-as-Grass was eating and not being eaten.

When the People sat by the burning logs during nighttimes, they often saw behind their eyes Tall-as-Grass lying on the ground and the Bad One licking his foot. None of the People had seen this before. Why didn't the Bad One eat the foot? Tall-as-Grass was happy that it didn't. Soon the foot became the same size as the other one and no longer left red marks on the ground. Now Tall-as-Grass ran away from the Bad Ones when they came out of the grass to eat the People.

12. Hear My Tale about a New Bad One

The People did not stay long in one place. They were always walking, walking over open ground, through tall grasses, through many tree-homes, where the waters moved fast, where the waters waited, where the waters never came, where stones stung their feet, where branches grabbed their legs, and where they must not walk ever again.

The People were always looking for Bad Ones and there were many kinds of Bad Ones to look for. Some lived in the sky, some in the water, some in the tree-homes, and some on the ground where the People lived. One day the People met a new Bad One they did not see or smell. It was their feet that warned them.

One day the People were walking in tall grasses as the hot light in the sky was about to hide from the Bad Ones. The People wanted to hide from the Bad Ones too but not in the grasses. Many Bad Ones lived in the grasses and the People could not see them. The People smelled of fear and huddled together as they used their hands and bodies to make their way towards tree-homes or caves.

Then the People suddenly came to where there was a large circle of open ground within the grass. Their eyes widened, their lips moved to show their teeth and the footsteps in their chests felt heavy. The People did not look into each other's eyes as they often did to know what to do but instead ran into the open space to get away from the thick and tall grass were the were afraid.

Eyes-that-Water ran the farthest into the open space but then stopped as if she saw a Bad One hiding right in front of her. But she did not scream to warn others of a Bad One, she just stopped and looked down at her feet entering the wet ground. Eyes-that-Water tried to run to the other side of the space but her feet were held by the ground. The more she tried to run the more the ground ate her. She turned and looked with her stone-colored eyes at the others.

Some of them also were being slowly eaten by the wet earth. The People who stopped where the grasses ended and the open space began looked at the others being sinking into the ground. No one had ever seen this kind of Bad One before. No one knew what to do.

Good-Hider had not run far into the open space but he too was slowly sinking into the ground just as Eyes-that-Water was. He turned to look at the others and screamed as the People screamed when being eaten by Bad Ones. As he sunk into the ground, Good-Hider watched the People grow taller, and the grass too. He pushed against the ground with his hands but the ground gripped his hands as it had gripped his feet, and now his legs. Good-Hider did not know what to do.

Then he saw behind his eyes what the People do when a Bad One finds them in an open space where there is no place to hide. He bent over and put his face in the mud and his hands out in front of him. Sometimes Bad Ones do not eat what they do not chase.

When Good-Hider bowed to the ground, it released his feet. He was no longer being eaten. Eyes-that-Water tried to do what Good-Hider had done but too much of her body had been eaten already and there was not enough left to bend over to the Bad One. But the others saw what Good-Hider had done and did it too. When they bent over their feet would slowly come out of the wet ground. But now they were lying without moving on top of the Bad without moving. Then Blowing-Ground and Water-Jumper began to move like the Bad Ones with no legs or arms and as they moved they came closer to the People watching from the tall grasses.

The People fell to their knees and reached out their hands to grip the arms or legs of Blowing-Ground and Water-Jumper. Blowing-Ground and Water-Jumper did the same thing to the others who had bowed to the Bad One and were no longer being eaten. All the People were either pulling or crawling towards where the grass and open ground met. All except Eyes-that-Water. She was gone, except for her hands that were reaching up to grab the sky.

13. Hear My Tale about the Burning Friend

There was darkness outside the cave but inside the cave the darkness hid from the waving fingers of burning light. Even the darkness did not want to touch the friend of the People.

The People sat facing the burnings logs with their chins resting on their knees. Their eyes did not stop looking at the red, yellow, and blue colors moving one way and then another at the center of the circle made by the People. Sometimes they raised their heads to follow little pieces of light as they went up from the burning logs towards the top of the cave. Their noses smelled the logs becoming smaller and blacker. Their eyes blinked from the white cloud coming from the moving colors. The bodies of the People became warm like the logs and their chests moved in and out at the same time.

When the People closed their eyes they did not see the Bad Ones but caves with water, food hanging from tree-homes, and the running things that the People threw into the burning logs to make them taste good. Some also saw with their closed eyes another person sitting in the circle. The People moved from side to side like the tall grass when the wind walks through it.

Tall-as-Grass put one of his feet near the burning logs because heat was still a friend to his foot. Burning-Stick put his hands near the heat as his chin rested on his knees. He tried to catch the specks of light that were walking without legs to the top of the cave. Far-Cloud made a noise with his nose like the noise made by the Bad One with long hairs around its face. No one went outside the cave to get more logs or to make water. It was just heat and light and colors and the People.

The People were happy when they shared the cave with the friend that did not want to be touched. Their friend made the Bad Ones hide in the darkness and kept them from eating the People. Life was good when the People stayed near their friend and when their friend stayed near the People. The People could smell only the burning logs as the flames changed logs from the color of the People's hair to the color inside a dark cave.

The People did not smell or hear the Bad Ones moving towards the mouth of the cave. They were not big but they were many. Even the Big One that lives in a cave hides from them. The Bad Ones looked at the People sitting in the cave and showed their teeth.

Black-Cloud was following the small lights rising above her head when she saw the Bad Ones across the open ground outside the cave. She shrieked a warning. The People jumped up as if they were sitting on flames and looked out of the mouth of the cave. The Bad Ones were not hiding from the moving light. Their eyes ate the yellow of the burning logs.

Some of the Bad Ones looked up into the black sky and howled. The sound made the People run back and forth in fear and huddle together and push themselves into the hardness of the cave. Their skin became wet and their chests moved in and out as when they are chased up a tree-home by a Bad One. In the cave the People had no sharp sticks to wave or rocks to toss, only the heat and light that made other Bad Ones hide in the darkness.

Long-Arms jumped forward and picked up a burning log but he did not squeal. He put one foot after the other as if jumping and ran towards the Bad Ones and then tossed the burning log at them. They moved aside to make room for it but the log did not make them run away. Long-Arms stood still and then he turned to run back to the cave but the Bad Ones with yellow eyes chased him and caught him and ate him in front of the People. Nothing could be heard but the snarls and snaps made by the Bad Ones as they fought over the meat that once was Long-Arms.

Then Burning-Stick gripped a burning log and jumped out of the cave. The Bad Ones looked at him and wanted to eat him too. But Burning-Stick did not throw the burning log. He stood there and swung it back and forth as tree-homes move when the sky is filled with wind and noise. Pieces of light left the swinging log and went into the yellow eyes and black noses of the Bad Ones.

Water-Fall and Blowing-Ground saw what Burning-Stick was doing and they also grabbed burning logs and went to him. They did not throw the logs as Long-Arms had done but moved them back and forth as Burning-Stick was doing. They moved the sticks until their arms hurt and they wanted to stop but they did not stop. The moving logs got brighter and more yellow as they waved back and forth under the black sky. Each time they moved they made the same sound made by the Bad Ones that live in the sky when they fall towards the ground to grab food in their sharp feet. The stick swingers filled the black sky with many burning lights. The Bad Ones with yellow eyes turned away from the flaming logs and went back into the darkness. They ate no more People.

The People had to stay close to their burning friend and keep their burning friend close to them.

14. Hear My Tale of a New One

No-Hair was going to give the People a new one. The People looked for a place where the Bad Ones could not smell the new one or hear it cry. The People found a cave that looked down on the tops of the tree-homes. It was hard to get to and No-Hair could not climb to it on her own. The People had to push and pull her to where the darkness of the cave kept out the light in the sky.

Sign-Reader and Water-Fall and Eyes-that-Laugh went with No-Hair into the darkness of the cave. The others picked up logs and branches to burn. Black-Cloud brought to the logs and branches the skull that carried heat and specks of light, carrying it by placing a stick through its eye-holes. The friend of the People did not like to be touched.

No-Hair did not sit on the ground as when looking into the burning logs but sat as when making water. Her arms rested on her knees. Sign-Reader, Water-Fall, and Eyes-that-Laugh made a circle around her by holding hands, and they closed their eyes and made the sound that the wind makes when it touches the tree-homes. No-Hair did not look at them but at the ground beneath her.

Then she made white water and red water but she made no sound. Then out of her came first the head and then the body of a new one. No-Hair put her hands together to keep the new one from falling to the ground. The new one was wet and its color was like color inside a mouth. No-Hair held the new one close to her eyes and looked at the hands and feet and then at its face and eyes. The new one moved its arms and legs as the People do in deep water. No-Hair ran her tongue over its body. Then she gave it to Water-Fall to hold as she picked up the wet and soft, white and red things that came out of her along with the new one, and ate them.

The new one was passed from Water-Fall to Sign-Reader to Eyes-that-Laugh. They were happy to see that the new one would someday give the People more new ones. The new one made sounds like those made by the little sky-dwellers that rest in the tree-homes. The ears of the People outside the cave heard the sounds and moved among each other in circles and looked in each other's eyes and showed their teeth and made hoot noises. A new one was good for the People.

Outside the cave First-to-Shout walked into the darkness to find the new one. No-Hair saw him even in the darkness and handed the new one to him. He held it away from him in both hands and looked at it as if it was far away. He looked and he looked. Then he sniffed it all over as if his nose was trying to eat the new one. Then he handed the new one back to No-Hair and sat down on the ground beside her. The rest of the People came into the cave and touched the heads of No-Hair, First-to-Shout, and the new one.

No-Hair stood up and carried the new one to the burning logs. She held it near the heat until the hair of the new one was as dry as the ground inside the cave. Then she sat down at the burning logs and crossed her legs and held the new one to her chest to give it food. The new one ate and No-Hair moved back and forth like the grass when touched by the wind. She made low sounds to the new one that had no meaning, but the new one understood the sounds and made them back to No-Hair. Then No-Hair looked up at the People and made the sound that meant "quiet one." The People would call the new one *Shaaaheee*.

The People were happy. It was good to have a new one. It was also good to have a new one that the Bad Ones could not hear.

15. Hear My Tale about Wet Logs

Some of the People wanted to look for a new home. Others did not. They liked their cave with the hole in the top and the many tree-homes with food on their branches. But others pointed through the rocks and over the grass and made the sound *weeeahah* again and again. At nighttime they were the last to come back to the tree-homes and to the cave. Their faces looked unhappy. The People looked into each other's eyes and walked about and made sounds to each other but some still wanted to do one thing and some do another.

When the light circle came out of hiding the People who wanted to look for a new place stood in the open ground. They moved from leg to leg and made the sound *weeeahah* again and again. The others did not go to them. The ones who wanted to look for a new home turned towards the grass and began walking, but the others made the sound *aya* and *nakall*, "who does good for us." They did not make the sound *hooosa* because those walking were looking for a home for all the People not for some of the People. They would come back.

Cave-Finder, Sign-Reader, Night-Sky-Mover, Tall-as-Grass, Far-Cloud, and First-to-Shout walked through the grass. They stopped again and again to sniff the air and look into the sky for Bad Ones. But when they did not find tree-homes in the grass, they were afraid. When the circle of light became red and was starting to hide in the ground, the People looked for a place to hide also. Then the light circle showed them a tree-home and made it red. The People ran to it and grabbed the branches and climbed as high as they could. Some of them lay on their backs on the branches and some on their fronts. They were afraid that the Bad One with black spots would find them and climb up and eat them, but their eyes closed anyway.

Their eyes opened again when the circle of light came out of hiding. The People sniffed the air for smells of Bad Ones before they left the tree-home and went back into the tall grass. Their noses found no sign of Bad Ones so they dropped from the branches like soft food and began to walk again. The grass was so high and strong that the People had to push it with their hands and arms. Sometimes the grass ate their skin and made red water drip from fingers and hands, arms and legs. The People pushed on anyway. They looked into each other's eyes and saw that they were more afraid of returning to the cave than of going to the place they could not picture.

The light circle heated made the heads of the People hot as a rock and the People needed water. Their tongues were becoming bigger and their mouths could not make sounds. Then the People saw many tree-homes in the distance and the People now were not afraid anymore. But they still needed water. Then they saw low green grass hiding in the yellow grass and going into the tree-homes. The green grass was drinking water. The People ran to it and found what they needed. The People brought the water up to their faces in their hands and made licking sounds and sucking sounds. The water did not move fast but waited for them.

The People looked into each other's eyes and grinned and clicked their teeth. They were happy. The People had found tree-homes and had found water. They now began to look for a cave or high rocks. As they followed the water into the darkness of the many tree-homes, they smelled something strange. "?????" The People moved very slowly and did not make any noise. Their eyes went everywhere but it was into the darkness that they looked the longest. The People moved on slowly but then suddenly stopped. Their noses found a new smell. People? Burning logs? Water? When they stepped around a big tree-home, they found it.

Logs on top of logs lying in a circle on the ground. This is the way logs looked back at the cave of the People. But the logs were not burning. They were wet but hot. Sign-Reader bent over and smelled the ground and looked at the logs and at the footprints in the dirt around them. She made the sound of fear but made it low—*eevooorr*. The People did not move. Only their heads moved as they turned one way and another. Finally their eyes looked into the darkness and their ears went there too. They saw and heard nothing, but something had put water on burning logs.

The People walked backwards. Their heads turned from one side to the other and their eyes ran into the darkness to see who left this sign to the People. The footsteps inside them ran fast and hard. When they found again the place where they drank water they turned and ran into the tall grass. They ran and ran. Behind their eyes they saw the People waiting for them. They wanted to be back with them.

The light in the sky was about to hide from the Bad Ones when Cave-Finder, Sign-Reader, Night-Sky-Mover, Tall-as-Grass, Far-Cloud, and First-to-Shout again saw the cave of the People at the same time that the People at the cave saw them. The People climbed up the rocks and the People slid down the rocks. There was much hugging, kissing, touching, and purring.

After a time the People who had returned began shaking their heads. They made the sound of fear—*eevooorr*—and put logs in a circle. They all pointed and made their finger go into the sky back and forth and said *nakall*, the friend who did not want to be touched. They then shook their heads again and said *eewoo*, "water." The People who stayed in the cave looked at the circle of logs on the ground and then looked out over the grass to where the light was hiding from the Bad Ones and then looked at the faces of those who came back. But the People could not see behind their eyes why burning logs were made wet. Or who could such a thing.

16. Hear My Tale of the Earth Shaking

Some of the People in the cave were putting more logs into the flames while others slid down the smooth rock and sat in the open ground next to each other where they picked things from their hair. As they picked and ate the People made soft sounds to each other that did not mean anything but made the People felt good.

The People sitting on the ground outside the cave smelled nothing, heard nothing, saw nothing to make them afraid. Nothing but the noise made by the sky-dwellers as they all suddenly left their resting places in the tree-homes. There were so many of them that they made the circle of light go away. The People looked up at the sky-dwellers filling the sky and watched them go one way and then another. Was this a sign of a Bad One?

Then the People felt heat inside them and the heat made the hair on their bodies reach out. Some of the People tried to jump up as if they were getting ready to run but they could not run or even stand. Underneath their feet the ground began to walk and it made the People fall down like walking on a log in the river. At the same time they were falling the People heard noises like the sound of running water falling on rocks or the sounds of Bad Ones talking to each other at night. The People looked to the tree-homes and saw that even they could not stand up. They moved one way and then another and some fell to the ground. The People inside the cave made the sound of fear—*eevooorr*—as rocks fell on their heads and the cave itself shook from fear just as the People were shaking.

The People looked into each other's eyes to find out what to do. Those inside the cave wanted to run outside, those outside wanted to run inside. Suddenly grasses were filled with Bad Ones and the ones they chase, all running across the ground as the ground made dark caves under their feet and tried to eat them. The People ran up the rocks as fast as they could to join the People near the cave and to get away from all the things being chased through the moving tree-homes on the ground with its many mouths. The People held on to each other to keep from falling.

From the rock they looked out over the trees and saw a river coming at them through the tree-homes as fast as if falling from high rocks. It roared like the Bad Ones with long hair around their heads. The People did not have time to look into each other's eyes to find out what to do. They just ran as far inside the cave as they could.

Outside the opening of the cave a noise like a great rock falling into water hurt their ears and heads. Then their feet told them that the water was following them into their hiding place. But the water touched only their feet and soon it did not touch even them. The People hugged each other and smelled each other and moaned *hooosa* in shared pain and fear. No-Hair and her little one made their way back to the opening of the cave. The others followed.

Outside they saw below them things that made their eyes stare. They saw Old Ones crawling on the ground swinging their heads and tails back and forth just as the trees had move before the river came. They saw the Bad Ones without legs climbing up tree-homes. They saw other things lying on their backs with their feet sticking up at the sky. And they saw the body of Log-Bringer lying flat on the wet ground with soft dirt filling his mouth. Soon the Bad Ones would be coming back to eat those that could not move.

The People touched each other and hugged as they looked out to where the water had come at them. From now on the People would be afraid of its return. Water was good but so much water was bad. They had to be ready for it. But how? And how to be ready for the shaking of the ground and falling tree-homes and rocks? And where would they find the heat to make more burning logs?

The People were filled with fear as they sat down on the wet ground and rested their heads on their knees.

17. Hear My Tale of Desire

The hot burning logs made the People see many things behind their closed eyes. Some saw the food that grows on tree-homes, some saw faces in water, some saw themselves eating meat from bones left by the Bad Ones, and some saw themselves hugging and touching one of the People. Behind his closed eyes Fast-Climber saw himself hugging and touching Water-Fall. And behind his closed eyes Water-Jumper also saw himself hugging and touching Water-Fall. Water-Fall behind her closed eyes saw herself hugging and touching a new one.

The People found many tree-homes with food. Some climbed up the tree-homes and gripped the branches and moved them back and forth until the food fell to the ground. The others picked up the food and pushed it into their mouths, making sounds with their lips like when their feet step into wet dirt. Fast-Climber gripped many branches and made a lot of food fall to the ground for the People to eat. He did not eat as much as the others but he was happy watching the others eat. Water-Jumper picked up some of the food and brought it to Water-Fall. She took it into her hands and ate it. The water from the food made her mouth and face wet, but her tongue caught as much water as she could.

Fast-Climber was on a branch high in the tree-home and looked down to see Water-Jumper feeding Water-Fall. This put a thorn inside him. His hair stood out and feet were kicking in his chest. He let go of the branch and fell to the ground near Water-Fall and Water-Jumper. Then he swung at the food in Water-Jumper's hands and made it fall to the ground. He jumped on it as if it were a running thing with long ears. This made Water-Fall turn and run towards the cave. The others stopped eating and looked to where Water-Jumper and Fast-Climber were screeching like the sky-dwellers with long arms. Their hair stood up and their eyes became small. They showed their teeth as they moved around each other making their legs long.

Far-Cloud and Strong-Branches and Night-Sky-Mover and Cave-Finder all made the sound *oooah*. They walked towards Water-Jumper and Fast-Climber and said *oooah* with each footstep. Night-Sky-Mover and Cave-Finder gripped the arm of Fast-Climber and pulled him back towards the tree-home he jumped from. Far-Cloud and Strong-Branches stood in front of Water-Jumper and made the sound *shaahee*. Water-Fall stopped running and turned to look at what the People were doing. Fast-Climber ran away from Night-Sky-Mover and Cave-Finder and ran towards Water-Fall. She stood still as she watched him run towards her. He grabbed her arm and turned back to look at the others.

They moved towards him and made the sound *oooah* over and over again. They looked into his eyes and put their hands on his arm and lifted it up like it was a log. Fast-Climber let his arm be lifted. His body was moving as if the little black things were crawling on it and his eyes were looking everywhere and his head moved as if he were seeing Bad Ones everywhere. The People moved closer to him and made the sound *hummmm* through their noses. They made the sound together and did not stop making it until Fast-Climber did not move his head back and forth and his body was not cold.

It was not good for the People to fear each other. The People were not the People when they did.

18. Hear My Tale about Fast-Climber

Fast-Climber sat among the People but he did not feel with the People. At the burning logs he closed his eyes and saw in the darkness Water-Fall, Water-Fall and Water-Jumper. He could see himself offering food to Water-Fall but he could also see her taking the food offered by Water-Jumper. This he saw in the darkness behind his eyes each time the light in the sky hid in the ground from the Bad Ones. He saw it again and again.

It came to pass that Fast-Climber no longer liked the taste of food, no longer liked the People, no longer liked Water-Fall, and no longer liked Water-Jumper. He felt as he felt when he smelled Bad Ones. He was afraid but he also wanted to throw rocks and swing sticks. His face looked like the face made he made when walking on sharp rocks. He could not click his teeth or curl back his lips. He did not rest his head on his knees but kept his head up as if he were looking for Bad Ones.

When the People climbed the rocks to get to the cave, Fast-Climber did not reach out a hand or foot to help anyone. When Quiet-One came near him he pushed her with his foot. When Sign-Reader yelled *oooah*, Fast-Climber dug his fingers into his hands and raised them over his head to make Sign-Reader back away. When Black-Cloud tried to hug him Fast-Climber pushed her away. When Blowing-Ground touched him to pick crawling things out of his hair, Fast-Climber screeched and jumped up. When Night-Sky-Mover came up to him and looked into his eyes, he spit water from his mouth into her face.

When the darkness came, Fast-Climber did not lie down with the People in a tree-home or cave but stood up in the branches and shook them or turned one way or another on the ground. Fast-Climber did not leave the cave to make water but made it where the People were sitting near the burning logs. Fast-Climber would walk among the People without looking at them. He would go into the darkness of the cave and hoot and make the sounds made by the Bad Ones that live in caves. He would go into the grass and not return to the People until the circle of light was in the sky many times.

Sometimes Fast-Climber made strange sounds that had no meaning to the People but sounded like the sounds made by the Bad Ones. Sometimes he placed his hands on the sides of his head and pressed as if he were trying to break open the food growing on branches. Sometimes he pulled the hair on his face until it came out. Sometimes he jumped on sharp rocks and put his tongue in the dirt. Sometimes he would run towards Water-Fall and make the sound *eevooorr!* Sometimes he would walk in circles around Water-Jumper without moving his eyes away from him.

Fast-Climber was unhappy with the People and the People were unhappy with Fast-Climber. They no longer wanted him to be one of them. The People no longer touched Fast-Climber, or looked him in the eyes, or made sounds in his ears, or huddled next to him when the People sat looking at the burning logs. When the People looked for food, they stayed away from where Fast-Climber was looking for food. When they found food they did not give him any, and he had to find his own food. Water-Fall kept away from him.

Then one day the People did not let Fast-Climber come back with them to the cave. They yelled *oooah* and looked at him with eyes used to look at a Bad One. Black-Cloud and Burning-Stick and First-to-Shout picked up sticks and stones and stood with them in their hands looking at Fast-Climber. He jumped up and down and turned in circles with his arms out and made the sound *hooosa*. When he looked at the many eyes that were looking at him, they said the same thing. Fast-Climber turned his back to the People and pounded the ground with his feet as he walked into the tall grass and away from Water-Fall and the People.

19. Hear My Tale of the Stingers

The People liked to eat meat but they also liked to eat the food that hangs from the branches of tree-homes and bushes, and the food hidden inside the soft caves made by the yellow and black things that *buzz*. This food made the mouth grip the tongue and the lips press together as when the People kiss. The People always looked for this food when they were walking.

One day the People found hanging in a tree-home the little soft cave where the yellow and black stingers lived. Strong-Branches climbed to it. He pushed his hand through a hole, moved it around, and then pulled it out with yellow mud clinging to it. He put his fingers into his mouth and rubbed his fingers with his tongue. Strong-Branches did this again and again. The People on the ground made the sound *eeookos*, wanting to join in the pleasure.

Strong-Branches then pulled on the soft cave until it came loose from the branch and fell to the ground. The cave broke open. Soon the air was filled with stingers from broken cave on the ground and also from other caves hanging in other tree-homes. The People now were stung all over their bodies, on hands, arms, backs, legs, and heads. The People slapped at the stingers but more of them kept coming from their caves in the tree-homes.

When the People climbed up into the branches, the stingers followed them and did not stop biting them no matter how high the People climbed. Some People swung their arms but this did not stop the little things from biting. First-to-Shout put his hands over his eyes and simply stood still and screamed. Others suddenly ran away without staying together and could not see where to put their feet and ran into branches or fell over sticks on the ground.

The People did not stop running until they heard *oooah*! when the black and yellow things stopped biting and returned to their soft caves. The circle in the sky was going into the ground when all the People were together again.

All of them moaned in pain. Some had spots on them and some had big lips and closed eyes. All the People picked stingers from their hair but they did not put them in their mouths to eat. Hair-on-Face lay on the ground and did not move. His body was filled with water. His one arm could not keep away the stingers that wanted to bite him. Hair-on-Face was finally lost to the People. It was not a Bad One that took him but the black and yellow stingers that made the food that made the People want to kiss. As the People looked at Hair-on-Face they could see that now he was being eaten by the crawling little black things that eat everything until all that's left are white bones.

The People did not know what sound to make.

20. Hear My Tale about Bad Ones Eating

The People heard sounds that always made their hair stand up and their skin crawl. The Bad Ones were trying to eat something that did not want to be eaten. The air was filled with roars and howls and snorts and bellows. The sounds were near.

The People ran from the cave to the edge of the rock and looked down towards the open ground were a circle of Bad Ones were trying to bite a grass-eater. This grass-eater was as big as the rocks the People crawl over to get to the cave. It had long white branches coming from its head and the branches looked like arms that wanted to hug. All of the Bad Ones were not as big as the grass-eater.

The grass-eater moved its head back and forth but the Bad Ones did not want to be hugged and they jumped away. They were trying to put their teeth into the legs of the grass-eater and climb on its back, as the People climb on the back of big rocks when they climb to the cave. The grass-eater turned one way and then another and then in circles, making the dirt rise into the sky. It kicked when the Bad Ones tried to bite its legs, and its nose made blowing sounds and its red tongue hung from its mouth. It moved its head one way and then another to see all the Bad Ones lunging and biting at it.

One and then another of the Bad Ones jumped on the back of the grass-eater and bit into it and then jumped off. They dug their claws into it and made red water flow, and tried to bite and claw its kicking legs. As the People watched, the grass-eater began to make more and more noise with its nose and did not kick as much. Its legs were shaking like the legs of a new one.

The People watched as a Bad One with hair around its face bit into a back leg and did not let go. The leg could not move. The grass-eater turned to grab the Bad One in its arms but it couldn't reach it. Another Bad One jumped onto the back of the grass-eater and bit into its neck and then another bit into its throat and did not let go. The snorts became harder for the People to hear. Then the grass-eater put its front knees on the ground and rolled over and made a sound as when the wind moves through the tree-homes. Its eyes were trying to see the Bad One biting into its neck but it could not. Its tongue almost touched the ground, and red and white water rolled down it into the dirt. The Bad Ones began to eat the grass-eater before its legs stopped kicking.

The People looked and did not move. The Bad Ones were good at eating. No grass-eater could run fast enough or was big enough to keep from being food for them. The People were afraid of the Bad Ones but they could not stop watching them. The Bad Ones did not eat all the meat and would leave some for the People, so they watched and waited. One and then another of the Bad Ones left the meat and bones and went back into the grass. Soon the meat was alone and waiting for the People, but other Bad Ones came out of the grass to eat it. Many came. These Bad Ones ate even the bones, and left nothing for the People.

Sign-Reader stood up and put rocks into her hands. She tossed them up into the air. Then Blowing-Ground did it and so did Water-Fall, First-to-Shout, and then the rest of the People. The sky was filled with falling rocks. When the Bad Ones lifted their heads to smell the People, many of the rocks hit them in the nose and eyes. The People hooted and jumped as they tossed the rocks into the air, and the Bad Ones howled and yelped and ran into the grass. They left meat for the People to eat.

Cave-Finder and Water-Jumper slid down the rocks to grab the meat left for them. Others followed but some were too afraid. The grass-eater was big and there was much meat left on its bones. The People stuffed the meat into their mouths. The taste of meat was good even when not taken from burning logs. Cave-Finder and Water-Jumper and the others put meat in their hands and around their neck to take back to those in the cave. Meat that fell from their hands ws left on the rocks.

It was good for the People to be afraid of the Bad Ones but not too afraid. It was good to stay away from the Bad Ones but not too far away. The People had to understand many things to stay alive.

21. Hear My Tale about Fog

One day the People opened their eyes but they could not see beyond their hands. Those in the tree-homes could not see the next branch. Those in the cave could not see where to put their feet. The People were too afraid to move. They called to each other and made the sound *eevooorr*. The hair on the People was too wet to stand up but it wanted to. If the People could not see the Bad Ones, could the Bad Ones see them?

The People used their tongues to taste the water on their face. It tasted like the wet air made by fast water when it falls on to rocks. The moving air made their skin shiver because the People could not feel the heat from the circle in the sky. The People were not afraid but their chests went up and down and feet were running inside them. Not being able to see in lighttime felt like finding a new cave.

Then Night-Sky-Mover shouted *heeheeah*! Others crawled their feet towards her voice. She was outside the cave and was pointing to where the People in the tops of the tree-homes floated in the air. Others in the tree-homes could not be seen at all but could be heard. Soon the People at the cave could see the People in the tree-homes gripping branches and they could see the People at the cave. The air was filled with hoots of happiness.

Little by little the People could feel the heat from the circle in the sky on their heads and backs. Their hair lost its wetness and their skin did not shiver. The People in the tree-homes sniffed the air for signs of the Bad Ones and when they did not find any, they climbed down to the ground and then up the rocks towards the cave. But the rocks were wet and the People's hands and feet did not stay where the People put them, and so some of the People slid back to the ground.

The People had to push and pull each other to reach the cave. Their chests went in and out as they crawled like the little black things that live in holes in the ground. Then Water-Jumped stopped and looked into the eyes of those gripping the wet rocks, and began to make short hooting sounds and click his teeth and pull back his lips. The others began to do the same. The People at the cave joined them in hooting and clicking teeth and pulling back their lips, but they also jumped up and down on top of the rocks. There was no fear in the People but happiness.

22. Hear My Tale about a Storm

The hair of the People stood up but the People could not smell or see any Bad Ones. Still the hair stood up. When the People touched each other their fingers made a little fire that stung, and above their heads the sky-dwellers hid themselves in tree-homes. The People looked at each other and made the sound *woo-ong* 'what is happening?'

Then their ears heard a low growl coming through the air. The People looked over the tops of the tree-homes as far as their eyes could go. Blackness was making the circle of light hide in the ground but this blackness was making its own light. This light was jumping from the sky into the ground where the light circle was now hiding. The sky became darker as the lights jumped faster and the growls became louder. The hair on the People stood up but the People didn't move. Their eyes would not look anywhere but at the burning light jumping from the sky to the ground.

Suddenly the tree-homes began to bend towards the People outside the cave. Dirt from the open ground climbed up the rocks and bit the eyes of the People, and with the dirt came branches and leaves from tree-homes. The sky became nighttime black. Next water came down from the sky and hit the People like sticks.

The People shouted the alarm *ehe ehe ehe* as they ran inside the cave until the dirt and branches and falling water could not follow them. They fell to the ground and huddled together. *Woo-ong? Woo-ong?* The People covered their ears with their hands to keep out the loud sounds. Even in the darkness of the cave the People shut their eyes as they do when Bad Ones find them alone in the open. Sometimes it was good not to see.

The People were cold and wet like the cave. The logs no longer burned and the People could not see the *aanaa* that held heat. This made them even colder, and afraid to leave the cave. But then the People heard something inside the cave that made them turn their eyes and ears towards the darkness behind them. It was the sound of a Big One but there was no Big One in this cave.

Suddenly out of the darkness came water as high as a person and moving as fast as a grass-eater when chased. Water came into the cave where light once did, and the water now wanted to join the water outside the cave as fast as it could. The People screamed and ran towards the mouth of the cave but the fast water caught them and carried them outside and it took some of the People over the rocks. The People screeched and screamed louder than the black sky. *Hooosa! Hooosa! Hooosa!*

Finally the sky became brighter and water stopped stinging their skin. Those who were not pushed over the rocks crawled to the edge and looked down. They saw Black-Cloud, Eyes-that-Laugh, First-to-Shout, Blowing-Ground, and Night-Sky-Mover gripping branches or hiding in crevices. Black-Cloud, Eyes-that-Laugh and the others looked up and clicked their teeth and made their lips curl.

But the new river from the cave had taken some of the People all the way to the ground. The others looke down at them, and saw that they too were looking up and clicking their teeth and making their lips curl. Because the water had made the ground soft and wet, there would be nothing for the Bad Ones to eat. The People made fast hoots and grunts because they were still the People.

23. Hear My Tale about Sickness

The hunger inside the People made loud growls. They left the cave and walked through tall grasses and many tree-homes to find something to eat.

They found small soft things hiding in bushes and picked them with their fingers and put them into their mouths as they picked them. They were so hungry that they didn't care if the bushes stung their hands and arms. Then the People chased things running on the ground and jumped on them or grabbed them with their hands or feet. Sometimes it took more than one person to get them.

Even things that the People did not eat looked like food now. Crawling things that were too little to grab were licked up, and logs turned over so the People could eat what was growing under them. The People ate things that moved and that did not move, white things, black things, red things, things soft and things hard, things big and things little, things that bit back and things that didn't. Hunger made the People wanting to eat anything, except other People.

This day the People ate as much as they could to feed the growling hunger inside them. It was not long before their bodies became bigger and moved slower. The People began to sit down on the ground and their eyes wanted blackness to come. They had eaten so much that did not sniff the air for the Bad Ones or see behind their eyes the cave of the People.

People who were sitting on the ground fell over and lay in the dirt, and some moaned when they made black water from where they sat. Others turned over and over on the ground with their hands grabbing the hair at the middle of their body. A few bent over and grabbed their legs and moved back and forth as they spit things out of their mouths--red things, black things, white things, and green things.

The People could not run or even walk. They were like the crawling things found under logs, lying on the ground ready to be eaten. Only Burning-Stick and Sign-Reader and Tall-as-Grass could stand up and sniff the air for signs of the Bad Ones. The rest of the People had too much pain to be afraid of being eaten. Some wanted to be eaten to end the pain.

The People were not happy. They wanted to be back in the cave, sitting around burning logs and licking cool water off the rocks of the cave and seeing behind their eyes the Bad Ones rolling on the ground and making black water from their rears too.

24. Hear My Tale about Bone Games

The People liked to play with bones they picked up from the ground. They tossed them in the air and sometimes at each other, turning in circles and then letting the bone fly out of their hand. They ran back and forth between each other making short hoot sounds with their lips wide and folded back and tossing bones here and there. Bone tossing made the People happy. Even Quiet-One did it.

The bones tossed into the air came down like white sky-dwellers coming to rest in the tree-homes. The bones came down on heads and backs and arms and even legs and feet. Sometimes the People jumped on the bones to hear them crack and break. Sometimes they tossed them on to rocks to make the sounds made by little sky-dwellers. Big bones made their sounds and little bones made their sounds. The People liked to listen to them.

It happened that one day Eyes-that-Laugh and Cave-Finder tossed bones at each other as they made their way back to the cave with the others. Eyes-that-Laugh was far ahead of Cave-Finder who tossed a bone at her as far as he could. Eyes-that-Laugh picked it up and ran inside the cave to toss it at Cave-Finder as he climbed up over the rocks. She hid behind a rock coming out of the ground that was shaped like a tooth. She tapped the bone against this rock as she waited to toss it, and the sound went into the cave and came back out again.

To Eyes-that-Laugh, this sound was better than the sounds made by bones when they were tossed against the rocks outside the cave. She tapped the bone against the tooth rock again, and the sound went into the cave and came back out again. Her ears like this sound more than the sounds made by bones when they were tossed against the rocks outside the cave. She made the sound again and again.

Cave-Finder saw where Eyes-that-Laugh was tapping the rock in the cave and ran to her and fell on his knees next to her. He listened and his lips pulled back and curled. He clicked his teeth and looked into her eyes but her eyes were almost closed as if it was nighttime. Others came into the cave to listen to the sounds that Eyes-that-Laugh was making with the bone. They watched her tap it against the rock again and again. They heard the sound go into the cave and come back.

Cave-Finder touched Eyes-that-Laugh with one hand and reached out to her with the other hand palm up and leaned his head to the left, as the People do when asking for food. Eyes-that-Laugh put the bone in his hand and moved back from tooth rock. Cave-Finder pushed the bone against the rock and it made the dull sound a rock makes when it falls into dirt. Eyes-that-Laugh made short hoots and shook her head and then moved the bone in Cave-Finder's hand so that his fingers were holding it at one end. She made the motion in the air of tapping the rock and then nodded to Cave-Finder. He did what she showed him and made the sound that the People wanted to hear. It gave their ears more pleasure than the cracking sound made by jumping on bones.

Cave-Finder made the new sound again and again in time with the footsteps inside his chest. Then others reached out their hands to him with their palms up.

The People had found a new pleasure from bones.

25. Hear My Tale about a Collision

The light circle was high and made the heads of the People felt hot and wet. Even the black shapes on the ground crawled away to hide. The People did not want to open their eyes or look up, but suddenly they had to.

A burning light ran across the sky and then hid behind the high rocks. It made a noise as when the sky becomes dark and hits the People with water, and the earth shakes, and rocks fall down inside and outside the cave. After the sound, the People saw dark clouds climbing to the sky from behind the high rocks where now many tree-homes were red and hot. This was good for the People.

They turned to look into each other's eyes. This thing was new and they wanted to see what it was, but they did not understand how far they would have to walk to see it. Suddenly Never-See-Me, Black-Cloud, First-to-Shout, Good-Hider and Sign-Reader formed a circle and hugged each other to tell the others that they would go. Only going there would tell them how far they had to go.

They walked towards where the light circle comes out of hiding. Light to light heat to heat. Never-See-Me, Black-Cloud, First-to-Shout, Good-Hider and Sign-Reader walked slowly and often stopped to sniff the air for signs of Bad Ones and to look at the grey air coming up from the ground. The grey air was still far away and they walked until the darkness made things grey and black. The People would have to spend the night in tree-homes, and would have to climb as high as they could. Once in the top branches, the People could see red light on the ground but it was not the light circle they saw. They could not close their eyes the whole night.

After they walked another lighttime and nighttime, the People could smell the burning tree-homes and feel their eyes make water. Then, finally, they saw many black and white tree-homes lying down on the ground giving smoke to the sky. The People stopped and turned their heads one way and another to see the burning thing that came from the sky. As they walked their feet were stung by the heat of the ground. Then Good-Hider sat on a log, gathered sticks and leaves lying on the ground, pushed then together, and then put one foot on them. He bent some sticks so that the leaves would not fall away. Then he did the same for the other foot. Never-See-Me, Black-Cloud, First-to-Shout and Sign-Reader watched what Good-Hider did for the first time and they did the same thing. Now the People could walk on the ground without their feet jumping in the air from the heat.

They walked until they saw tree-homes burning. They could not get close to the tree-homes and had to walk so that only one side of their bodies was hot. They came to rocks where they could see more, but what the climbed the rocks they did no see more. All their eyes saw a big hole with clouds of smoke in it. Sign-Reader made signs to the others that it would take the People another lighttime to walk from one side of the hole to the other.

The People did not want to walk that far. What they wanted was to see the burning thing that ran through the sky and made many tree-homes burn. Where had this thing come from? Where did it go? The more the People looked for it the more *huh?* lines were in their faces.

After lighttimes and nighttimes the People were back at the cave and tree-homes with the others, and they brought back as many burning logs as they could carry. They also brought back the pictures in their heads that they acted out for the others around the fire in the cave. Now everyone felt the fear of burning things falling from the sky.

26. Hear My Tale about Two

The People saw behind their eyes the hanging food their lips wanted to kiss. It was time to walk to the little trees where the red and yellow and green food hid under the leaves. The People gathered outside the cave and looked into each other's eyes. Should all the People go or some of the People go? No one wanted to stay because everyone tasted the food in their mouths already. They looked to Sign-Reader to lead them for she led the People to the right places and always away from the Bad Ones. She could do things that others could not do. The People followed her without fear.

Sign-Reader made the People walk where the grass was short and where there were no tree-homes. The People looked up to see the Bad Ones that made no sound as they fell from the sky and grabbed food in their stick hands. Sign-Reader walked fast towards the food of many colors. When the People saw behind their eyes the food hanging from branches, their mouths became wet without drinking water and they walked as fast as Sign-Reader.

The light circle was above their heads when Sign-Reader made the sound *heeheeah!* The People looked to where she was pointing and saw the food that was *eeookos*. The People ran to the branches and jumped into them to grab with their hands and mouths as much of the food they could find. Fast-Climber swung on the branches to make the food fall to the ground, and Night-Sky-Mover pulled down branches so others could eat. The People bit and pulled and tore and squeezed until they could not eat any more. They sat on the ground and grinned and hooted.

The circle of light in the sky was now going to its hiding place in the ground beyond the high rocks. It was time for the People to walk back to the cave and tree-homes. Sign-Reader got up and walked in front of the People pointing and making the sound *weeeahah*. The People gathered behind her and began stepping on the signs they had made walking to the food.

Suddenly Black-Cloud made the sound *nooaah!* The People stopped and turned to look at her. She ran and jumped among the People until she got to Sign-Reader and then turned and ran back to where she started. She looked into the eyes of all the People but she did not see Eyes-that-Laugh and Burning-Stick, and she made the sounds that made the People see what she saw. The People turned and looked at each other and made the sound *eevooorr* many times. Where was Eyes-that-Laugh and Burning-Stick? Had Bad Ones eaten them? Had they fallen into a hole or into the wet ground that eats People? The People made the *woo-ong* face. And the fear face.

Sign-Reader moved among the People saying the sounds for "Burning-Stick" and "Eyes-that-Laugh." Then the People also began to make the same sounds. Sign-Reader said the sounds louder and then so did the People. Then Sign-Reader climbed a tree-home and made the sounds by sucking in air and pushing it out. The sky-dwellers hiding in the tree-homes were afraid and jumped into the air. The People were also afraid and began to make the sound *hooasa*. Their eyes began to make water.

The People were making so much noise that only Quiet-One could hear the sound *aya* coming from among the tree-homes. She put her hands on both sides of her mouth and made many hoot sounds. The People saw what she was doing and stopped making the sounds for "Burning-Stick" and "Eyes-that-Laugh." Now their ears could also hear the sound *aya* coming from the darkness. Quiet-One did not stop hooting.

The sounds from the darkness became louder. Only the People made this sound. Then the People could hear branches snapping and then see branches moving. They were being moved by Eyes-the-Laugh and Burning-Stick. The People watched as they walked towards them. The faces of Eyes-that-Laugh and Burning-Stick were not afraid but happy as they looked into each other's eyes and grinned. Then they looked at the People and made the sound *eeookos!* The People nodded and grinned back at them, and then they all followed Sign-Read back home.

27. Hear My Tale about Water-Fall

The circle of light once again opened the eyes of the People. They opened their mouths and reached out their arms and made their bodies become stiff and longer. From cave and tree-home they called out to each other *aya aya* and then made their way to the open ground. Some of them pointed towards the tree-homes with food hanging from the branches and made the sound *weeeahah*, 'let's go to that place." The People sniffed the air and looked into the sky for signs of Bad Ones and then began to walk over open ground to find the soft food.

They walked a few steps when Water-Jumper stopped and made the sound of fear—*eevooorr*. The others stopped too. They looked up at the sky and into the grasses for signs of the Bad Ones but Water-Jumper was not looking at these places but at the People. His eyes went from one face to another. And then he made the sound of pain, *hooosa*. The People looked at Water-Jumper and made the face "?" Water-Jumper turned in circles as his eyes went over all the People and then he made the sound for "Water-Fall." The People looked at each other and also made the sound for "Water-Fall." There was no Water-Fall with the People.

Where was she?

Did the Bad One with black spots take Water-Fall during the darkness? The People began to say *hooosa* and bow their heads, but Water-Jumper bowed his head to look at the

101

ground. He walked in circles looking for where the Bad One put its feet. He looked for where the Bad One made red water come from Water-Fall. He looked for where the Bad One dragged Water-Fall. But Water-Jumper found no signs of a Bad One. What he found on the ground were signs of feet.

He called to the People *heeheeah*! They ran to him and their many feet almost made the signs go away. Water-Jumper yelled *oooah*! and the People stopped next to him. He leaned over and pointed with his finger at the signs in the dirt. Two people. Two people walking away from the cave and towards the grasses. Two people and something else. Two lines in the dirt. Were two People dragging logs? Why did Water-Fall drag a log? And who was walking with Water-Fall?

Sign-Reader bent over and now put her eyes and nose close to the ground. She looked and looked and sniffed and sniffed at the signs in the dirt. Then she stood up and pointed a finger at the foot prints and made the sound *ishsee*—'bad ones.' The faces of the People said "?" What Bad Ones walked with the feet of the People? What people were Bad Ones?

Sign-Reader then pointed a finger at the two lines in the dirt between the footprints. She made the sound for "Water-Fall." Again, the faces of the People made the sign "?" When did the feet of Water-Fall become logs? Sign-Reader did it all again. The People watched but made no sounds. Finally Sign-Reader dragged one of her feet in the dirt and the People said *hah*!

The People began to hoot and growl. Now they no longer saw behind their eyes the food hanging from branches but instead they saw Water-Fall being dragged through the dirt by two people. But what People were taking Water-Fall away? Sign-Reader and Water-Jumper began to follow the signs into the grasses and the People followed. They hooted and listened for other hoots, but no hoots returned to them.

The signs were easy to follow. The tall grasses were pushed to the ground where Water-Fall had been dragged by two people. The People followed the signs until the bright circle in the sky was near its hiding place in the ground and the People began to feel fear. It was the time when the People could not see the Bad Ones but the Bad Ones could see them. The People said *oooah* and stopped, looking into each other's eyes and sensing that it was time to go back to the high cave and tree-homes.

The People turned and walked back over the grasses they had pushed to the ground. But Water-Jumper did not walk fast because he wanted to follow the signs left by Water-Fall. Sign-Reader gripped his arm and pulled him so he would not be lost to the People as Water-Fall was lost. Sometimes the feet of Water-Jumper made the same log marks in the dirt as the feet of Water-Fall.

28. Hear My Tale about Crawling Things

The light circle was going to rest in the ground so the People wanted to rest too. But they had just found tree-homes filled with red, yellow, and green food and they began to eat. They made the kissing face with their lips and water dropped from their mouths as they hooted and grinned.

The People had many tree-homes to pick from. Some of the People picked from one tree-home, some from another, and the rest from yet another. It was hard for the People to see each other when they were picking in so many places, but no one had to beg for food because there was enough for all. There was so much food that the People threw on the ground what they could not eat.

On the ground the food was eaten by many little things that lived there. These things covered the food and sometimes took it away to their homes. The People did not look at these little things but at the food hanging from the branches of the tree-homes.

Suddenly, the food on the ground became black because of all the little things crawling over it. The People looked down at the ground and saw that even the dirt was black with crawling things, and they were covering the feet of the People and climbing up their legs. The People liked to pick and eat the crawling things but this time there were too many to eat. Now there so many that crawling things that they were eating the People.

The People pushed and hit and pressed down on the little black things crawling over them but the black things kept crawling biting them all over their bodies. The People jumped into the tree-homes to hide but they took many of the biters with them. In the tree-homes, the People helped pick black crawlers out of their hair, but they could not pull out the heads of the little black things once they had bitten. The heads did not stop biting.

The People began to feel fear when they saw grass-eaters of all kinds running out of the darkness of the tree-homes. Big grass-eaters and small grass-eaters tried to jump over the many black things covering the ground but each time they landed, more black things bit into them. The eyes of the jumpers were big with fear. The People looked into the darkness and saw why the grass-eaters were afraid.

What the People saw in the darkness coming through the tree-homes was a river of black biting heads. The river covered everything that did not run fast enough. A Bad One with no arms or legs was covered by little things and soon made into a long string of white bones. The river was moving as fast as the People could run and was as wide as a fallen tree-home. *Eevooorr! Eevooorr!* Now the fear of the People made their hair stand up and the feet inside them jump jump jump.

The black things did not crawl up the tree-homes to eat the People because they had food on the ground. But what if there was no more food on the ground? The light circle was now hiding in the ground and the People made the sound *hooosa* and then *weeeahah weeeahah*. The People wanted to leave the tree-homes and go back to the cave. The little black things did not eat rocks.

The young ones were put on the backs of strong runners and pushed their hands and feet into their hair. The People then dropped from the branches like they were food. Sign-Reader led them through the darkness. They ran and ran, but they could not tell when their feet were stepping in the river of biting things or on the ground. And they did not care. Behind their eyes all they saw were the big rocks they had to climb to get into the cave. The feet inside their bodies were running as fast and as hard as the feet at the end of their legs. They ran until their noses could smell old burnt logs and all the many smells the People left at the cave. When they reached the rocks and the tree-homes near the cave the People hooted and whooped and hugged and kissed Sign-Reader.

Some black things had fallen off as the People ran but others stayed in their hair. The People fell to the ground and rolled back and forth back and forth until their hair was filled with dirt, but others slapped and rubbed their hair and skin until they could not feel stings. The People waited for the light circle to come back into the sky before they could pick the black heads left in their skin.

The crawlers were small but when there were many of them, they ate what they wanted. The People saw behind their eyes little black things eating even the Bad Ones.

29. Hear My Tale about Stinger Friends

The People walked among the many tree-homes turning over logs to find things to eat. They found things with many legs that crawled on the ground and they found things that did not move and were soft in the mouth. The People bent over and kept their eyes close to the ground, but their noses liked to be there too because the ground had many good smells. They grabbed and picked and brought things to their mouths as fast as their fingers could move.

But none of the People smelled the Bad One that was crawling towards them through the grass. It was the one with spots that could climb. The Bad One pushed itself almost flat on the ground, and moved its ears but not its staring eyes. Suddenly it jumped through the air and ran towards the closest People, who did not have time to scream. Some fell away from the Bad One, some ran into the green darkness and some climbed up the tree-homes.

The Bad One tried to grab Night-Sky-Mover but she fell to the ground, crawled under a big log and ran up a tree-home. The Bad One turned in a circle to find another person to eat but the People were hard to find in the darkness. Except for those in the tree-homes. The Bad One looked up and saw the People huddled together above its head. It jumped up and began to climb towards them.

Now the People had time to scream. They gripped branches and climbed higher. So did the Bad One with the black spots. First-to-Shout, Good-Hider, No-Hair, Far-Cloud looked down at it and then looked up at the last branches of the tree-home just above their heads.

Strong-Branches was in another tree-home but he was screaming with the People. Suddenly he saw behind his eyes the time when the stingers filled the air and bit the People. And then he saw behind his eyes the stingers biting the Bad One. Strong-Branches saw in a tree-home next to his the cave home of stingers. He reached out and grabbed a branch and then let his body swing to the new tree-home. He climbed higher to where the stingers hide and pulled their cave free from the branch holding it. He could hear the zzzzzzz sound of the stingers inside. Some were still coming into it and some going out of it but they didn't bite him. Strong-Branches held the soft cave full of stingers as he went lower in the tree-home.

Strong-Branches looked over at the other tree-home and saw the Bad One reaching out to grab Good-Hider.

Strong-Branches saw behind his eyes his hand tossing the cave of stingers at the Bad One. The People in the tree-home were still shrieking but Strong-Branches was now silent and his eyes looked big at the Bad One and his eyes did not move. He gripped the tree-home with his legs and arm and then leaned towards the Bad One in the other tree-home. He swung the cave of stingers back and forth as if he were about to throw a bone.

The Bad One turned its head to look at what Strong-Branches was doing and tried to hit the cave home with its hand but its hand broke into the home of the stingers and stayed there. It stayed there even when the Bad One waved its hand in the air. As the Bad One shook the cave stuck on its hand, stingers soon filled the sky. They bit the Bad One again and again as they had once bitten the People. They bit its nose, its eyes, its lips, its tongue, its ears.

The Bad One turned and jumped down to the ground with the cave still on its hand. The stingers followed it to the ground. The Bad One ran into the darkness of the tree-homes jumping one way and then another and making the sound made by a new one. Many stingers followed him because they wanted their home back.

The People watched but did not move until the stingers went away. The People were happy that the stingers had filled the air and made the Bad One run away before it could eat any of the People. The People were also happy that Strong-Branches had made stingers friends of the People. Another new thing.

30. Hear My Tale about Strong-Branches

The People were happy that Strong-Branches tossed the stingers at the Bad One who climbed tree-home. Strong-Branches was happy too, and often saw what he had done behind his eys, and each time he saw it he felt strong.

So strong that he became a different Strong-Branches. When the People were looking for things to eat Strong-Branches would point and make the sound *weeeahah! weeeahah!* and then walk to where he pointed. If no one followed him, he would come back and grab some People by the arm and pull them or push them to where he pointed. The People would go but they were not happy. When anyone found food, Strong-Branches put out his hand with the palm up to ask for some. Soon Strong-Branches stopped finding his own food and ate the food of others without placing his palm up.

Strong-Branches no longer brought back logs for burning but pushed others towards where the logs lay on the ground. The People went to get the logs but they were not happy. When someone was hitting the rock inside the cave with a bone to make sounds, Strong-Branches would stick out his hand with the palm up and ask for the bone so he could make the sound. When the person held on to the bone, Strong-Branches would pull it from the hand of the other person. When someone held out a hand with the palm up to get the bone from him, he would use the bone to hit the hand. Strong-Branches often picked up the food placed in the burning logs and ate what he wanted. He pushed others out of the way to lay where he wanted. He walked among the People often making the sound zzzzzzzz.

The People were no longer happy with Strong-Branches. They did not like it when one person told the others where to find food or where to close their eyes at nighttime. They did not like it when one person took things from another. The People began to look into each other's eyes and to grunt and to make the face of pain and anger. Slowly the People began to turn away from Strong-Branches and not look at him.

When he put out his hand with the palm up, the People made their eyes look at the ground or the sky. When Strong-Branches pushed or pulled, the People walked a few steps and then sat down or hid. When Strong-Branches wanted to touch someone, the person turned away and walked fast. When the People were looking for food, they would look for food as far away from Strong-Branches as they could. This happened many times.

It came to pass that when the People opened their eyes, they saw Strong-Branches sitting outside the cave with his head bent down and his eyes looking at the ground. Strong-Branches no longer felt strong. He no longer wanted to push or pull any of the People. The People slowly came together and stood in front of him looking at him. He raised his eyes and looked back at them. His face said *hooosa*.

The People slowly made a circle around him and they touched him as he sat with his head down. Suddenly he felt strong in the old way. He was again among the People and not high in a tree-home looking down at them. He stopped walking among them making the sound zzzzzzzz. The People were happy again with Strong-Branches, and he was happy with them.

31. Hear My Tale about Two New Ones

Blowing-Ground was too big to hide in tree-homes when the darkness chased the circle of light from the sky. Her front rubbed against the branches and she did not like to climb high any more because when she looked down the ground moved up and down and back and forth. Her eyes lost themselves in her head and she didn't know which branch to grab because they moved when she reached for them. The tree-homes were no longer good for her. When the nighttime came Blowing-Ground could only stay in the cave. Even the cave was hard for her to climb to. The People had to lift her and push her as her front pushed back against the rocks.

Blowing-Ground did not walk around with the People but sat in the cave and held the front of her body. She moved her body back and forth slowly and made the sound *ahhh ahhh*. At nighttime she would put her back against the hardness of the cave while the others were on the ground. Blowing-Ground was given food to eat but sometimes the food came back out of her mouth. She was not happy.

The others touched her and rubbed her and picked crawling things out of her hair. This made Blowing-Ground stop moving back and forth and making the sound *ahhh*. She would look into the eyes of those touching and rubbing her and she would pull back her lips and click her teeth.

It came to pass that during the darkness Blowing-Ground made the sound *hooosa*. Water and red water came out of her and made the ground wet. Sign-Reader, Far-Cloud, Eyes-that-Laugh came to her and lifted her up. Blowing ground then spread her legs and let her backside go towards the ground. She looked down between her legs and watched a new one come from her. She did not yell or scream but made the sound *ahhh*. It is best not to tell the Bad Ones that there is a new person. Her arms were being held by Sign-Reader and Far-Cloud but the new one did not fall to the ground because Eyes-that-Laugh put her hands under it and caught it.

Blowing-Ground did not stop looking between her legs and she still made the sound *ahhh*. Then she saw another new one come out of her. Eyes-that-Laugh put her hands out to keep it from falling to the ground. Blowing-Ground gave the People new ones, and one of them would also give the People more new ones. She no longer felt pain but pleasure in her whole body. Sign-Reader and Far-Cloud helped her sit on the ground. They held the new ones and looked at them to make sure they were People. The new ones made short hoots and turned their bodies back and forth. Blowing-Ground picked up the things that came out of her with the new ones and ate them.

When they say another new one, the eyes of the People became big. They made a circle around Blowing-Ground and touched her and rubbed her and made the sound *aya aya*. Cave-Finder and First-to-Shout came into the cave and took the new ones to look at them and smell them. They looked and smelled and looked and smelled. Then each clicked his teeth in happiness. They gave the new ones to Blowing-Ground and she placed them on her body so both could get food at the same time. The People were stronger and happier. Blowing-Ground made the sounds for "Good Crawler" and "Good Follower." The People did not see behind their eyes the Bad Ones ever eating the new ones.

32. Hear My Tale about Watching Bad Ones

The People were afraid of the Bad Ones, but they were not afraid all the time. Sometimes the Bad Ones were not hungry and did not want to eat the People, so the People could watch the Bad Ones without fear. They watched them from the tree-homes or from high rocks, and could not take their eyes off them.

They saw that the Bad Ones are like the People. The Bad Ones eat things and they drink water, as the People do. The Bad Ones have red water inside them and bones. They have eyes and nose and mouth and tongue and teeth and legs and hands. They bring forth new ones and lick them and do not eat them. They live with others and do not eat them either. They lie on the ground and close their eyes. They sniff the air and they watch for things that move. They touch each other and hug. They make sounds to each other. They share food. Some Bad Ones even stand up and walk like the People.

Sometimes the People wanted to touch the Bad Ones and even hug them, but they did not. First-to-Shout tried to touch the Big One that walks like the People but the Big One did not want to be touched and hit First-to-Shout with the sharp sticks on his hand and gave him long red lines on his face and back that did not leave. After this no one tried to touch the Bad Ones even when they acted like People.

The People watched as Bad Ones chased food and fell from the sky with their sharp fingers in front of them to grab their food and take it far away. They watched as the Bad Ones made themselves into branches to fall on their food and made circles around it and then swallow it. They watched as the Bad Ones hid in the grass and moved without a sound as slowly as little black crawling things. They watched as the Bad Ones suddenly jumped and ran at grass-eaters and as the grass-eaters jumped and ran one way and then another way. They watched as the Bad Ones followed without a sound until one of the grass-eaters fell or was tripped. They watched as a Bad One bit the throat of the grass-eater until its legs stopped moving, and as others made the grass-eater into bones. The People watched when the Bad Ones went away so the People could find meat. And they watched to see how grass-eaters kept themselves from being eaten.

The People were afraid of the Bad Ones but the Bad Ones were always with the People. The People saw them behind their eyes when their eyes were closed or when their eyes stared into burning logs. The Bad Ones were part of the People. Sometimes the People wanted to be like the Bad Ones and not be afraid of them. But the People were not strong enough to touch Bad Ones or make them fear the People. The People had to fear the Bad Ones and watch them and not try to touch them even when they wanted to.

33. Hear My Tale of a Strange Body

The water inside the cave was going away but it was leaving behind a white circle on the rocks. The People licked the white circle and it tasted good but they wanted water more. There was no water coming through the hole in the cave and the water that did come out of the rocks no longer made a sound. The People had to find water, but it was hard to smell when there was little of it.

The People looked into each other's eyes. Should all the People leave the cave and look for water or only some of the People? Sign-Reader, Water-Jumper, Night-Sky-Mover, First-to-Shout, and Black-Cloud made the sound *eewoo*. They would look for water and the others would stay at the cave. When the circle of light came out of its hiding place, the water finders left the cave and walked into the tall grass. They stopped many times to sniff the air, not for water but for the smell of the Bad Ones. The Bad Ones had to drink water too.

Sign-Reader saw behind her eyes a big circle of water and she led the others towards it. But she did not see how long it would take to find it. The People walked slowly and stopped many times to lift their noses into the air. They were still walking when the circle of light became red and went into its hiding place in the ground to be safe from the Bad Ones that brought the darkness. That night the People did not find holes to hide in but tree-homes to climb during the darkness. They found branches to lie on as they looked up at the little lights in the sky put there by burning logs. Then their eyes went into darkness.

When the light came back into the sky, the sky-dwellers made sounds that went into the ears of the People and opened their eyes. The People pushed out their arms and legs as far as they would go and made them hard like branches. They opened their mouths and shut their eyes at the same time. Then they looked at the ground for Bad Ones. *Aya Aya* they said softly. The People dropped to the ground. Some turned in circles to find the way to walk to the water but Sign-Reader did not turn in circles but walked away from where the circle of yellow light was coming out of the ground, and the others followed her. The heat of the circle would be on their backs as they began to look for water again.

The light circle was high in the sky when the eyes of the People saw sky-dwellers making circles in the air. This was not a sign of water but a sign of meat. The People walked faster. The grass fell down before their feet until there was no more grass to fall. There in front of them was open ground with some tree-homes. They could still see the sky-dwellers making circles in the air but now the sky-dwellers were closer. Suddenly the ground was no longer flat but went down. The People could see the bright lights that water made. The lights were beneath them and far away. Why were the sky-dwellers not drinking?

The People made their legs and feet move fast towards the signs of water. The light in the sky looked into their eyes and this was a sign the darkness was coming. When they got to the circle of water they fell on the ground and put their heads into the water with their mouths open. They did not look for Bad Ones as the grass-eaters do when they drink water. The People saw nothing but the water.

When their mouths had no more room for water, some sat on the ground and some fell back to look at the sky-dwellers making circles in the air. *Huh?* What were the sky-dwellers looking at? The People stood up and made water and brown mud. Then Sign-Reader looked up at the sky-dwellers and began to walk towards them. The others followed Sign-Reader because she could see behind her eyes things others could not. The People stopped walking when the sky-dwellers made circles over their heads. Then Sign-Reader made the sound *oooah*! She turned and made the sound *heeheeah*! The People came up to her to look where she was looking at the ground. Their eyes became wide and white and did not move.

On the ground near their feet was something that looked like one of the People but was not one of the People. It was another. It was lying on the ground with its face in the dirt as if eating it. It did not move even though there were many little black and red and white things crawling over it. Sign-Reader got on her hands and knees to look at it. She blew in its ear but it did not move. She spit water in its face but it did not move. Black-Cloud rubbed its foot with her toes but it did not move. Night-Sky-Mover turned it over so that its eyes looked into the sky but the two white stones did not see the sky. Where did it come from? What was its name? Were there others? The People stood and looked and looked. They saw many things behind their eyes but their *huh* face did not go away. The more they saw the more their *huh* face became like rock.

This thing did not have any holes in it like the Bad Ones make when they eat. There were no white bones showing. Suddenly Sign-Reader pointed to the head of the thing where there was a black spot. *Huh?* What kind of Bad One would make only one black spot? What kind would not eat the thing? The People looked into each other's eyes but the *huhs* did not go away.

The People began to feel fear. Would their heads have holes in them for finding the circle of water? Would they fall on the ground and not move? Sign-Reader, Water-Jumper, Night-Sky-Mover, First-to-Shout, and Black-Cloud looked into each other's eyes and saw fear. They wanted to get back to the cave. Let the sky-dwellers eat this thing if they were not afraid to.

34. Hear My Tale about Telling the People

Sign-Reader, Water-Jumper, Night-Sky-Mover, First-to-Shout, and Black-Cloud climbed a tree-home near the water as the Bad Ones brought the darkness and the darkness brought the Bad Ones. The People could not make the darkness behind their eyes because their eyes would not close, so they lay on branches waiting for the light circle to return. They could still see the thing with a dark spot on its head. What was it?

Sign-Reader, Water-Jumper, Night-Sky-Mover, First-to-Shout, and Black-Cloud came down from the tree-homes even before the sky-dwellers made sounds. Sign-Reader walked towards the grey light and the others followed, their feet moving many times before they got back to the cave. When they reached the cave, Sign-Reader, Water-Jumper, Night-Sky-Mover, First-to-Shout, and Black-Cloud hooted and whooped their *eeookos* to the People waiting for them. The smell of burning logs filled the air.

The People jumped and grinned with pleasure. Then Sign-Reader used her arms and hands and feet to tell the People how far away the water was. The People stopped jumping and grinning, and looked into each other's eyes. They were afraid of walking in tall grass where the Bad Ones hid, and of walking until the Bad Ones brought the darkness. But going to the water would make the People feel even more afraid.

The water-finders looked into each other's eyes and they could see again what the sky-dwellers also saw. Then Sign-Reader fell face down on the ground and then Night-Sky-Mover got on her hands and knees and blew into her ear, but Sign-Reader did not move. Night-Sky-Mover looked up at the People, but they had the *huh* face. Then Night-Sky-Mover turned Sign-Reader over but Sign-Reader did not move. Night-Sky-Mover pointed to the head of Sign-Reader but the People still had the *huh* face. *Woo-ong? Woo-ong?* some of them said.

First-to-Shout, Black-Cloud, and Water-Jumper looked at each other, then Water-Jumper did something new. He went to a sharp rock growing from the ground and pressed his hand against it and pulled it back and did it again until red water came from his hand. Then he went to where Sign-Reader was on the ground, put his hand on the back of her head, and left it there until a circle of red could be seen on Sign-Reader's hair and skin.

Then First-to-Shout, Night-Sky-Walker, Black-Cloud and Water-Jumper pointed at the red spot and said *heeheeah heeheeah*! The People came nearer and looked at the red spot on Sign-Reader's head. First-to-Shout, Night-Sky-Walker and Black-Cloud said softly *eevooorr*. They said *ishsee* but with a *huh* face. The People who had not gone to the water were seeing many things behind their eyes. They saw that it was not good to go to the circle of water, Bad Ones or no Bad Ones.

35. A Tale of Going Back to the Water

The People were happy. They found food in the tree-homes, made sounds with the rocks with bones, picked crawling things out of their hair and ate them, pushed stones back and forth with the young ones, sat around the burning logs to warm their skin and made the footsteps inside their chests walk softly and slowly.

But behind their eyes the People often saw again and again Sign-Reader, Water-Jumper, Night-Sky-Mover, First-to-Shout, and Black-Cloud making sounds and pointing after they came back from finding water and something else that made them afraid. The People still could not see behind their eyes what was found by the water but after they looked into each other's eyes again and again, they all wanted to find what the others had found. They would walk to the circle of water together so all could see. Wanting to see was stronger than not wanting to see.

Even before the light circle returned, the People were walking off into the grass behind Sign-Reader who always walked in the right way. Out of fear the People hooted, hissed, growled, clicked their teeth, and pulled on branches as they walked because making noise gave the People strength and sometimes made the Bad Ones run away from the People. They walked until the light in the sky turned red and was looking into their eyes before as it went to hide for the night. This made the People want to hide too, but there were no caves but only tree-homes, and only a few of them.

The People filled them, with everyone tring to climb as high as they could because it was not good to be at the bottom during the nighttime. The Bad Ones could jump high, and the People dropped things through the branches during the night. When the People found their places, they purred and hummed and hooted softly to each other. Soon there was no sound but the rasp of sleep.

Sign-Reader was moving before anyone and she made the others move by hooting loudly and tossing sticks into the branches until the People came down to the ground. She pointed away from the new light and made her arm go up and over. Again she then began to walk and the People followed. Now they did not make noise because they wanted to sleep and their legs moved like branches. But they walked and walked anyway.

The light circle made their backs hot, then made their heads hot, and then made their faces hot. The light circle went from white to red and made the People close their eyes until they could see only the ground near their feet. Then before they could see it, they smelled water. They lifted their faces to see specks of light jumping back and forth on the water as if the water were burning.

The People forgot their fear and ran towards it. Their mouths were as dry as the dirt outside the cave. But Sign-Reader, Water-Jumper, Night-Sky-Mover, First-to-Shout, and Black-Cloud did not follow the People. They walked slowly to the place on the ground where the thing had been found. But the thing was gone, but it left its bones. The long bones were broken and the skull had a small hole in it. This was not a hole made by a Bad One. This hole was made by ????? Sign-Reader stood up and began to look all around, turning in a circle like the sky-dwellers do. She eyes were afraid.

The others lifted up their heads from the water and looked to where   Sign-Reader, Water-Jumper, Night-Sky-Mover, First-to-Shout, and Black-Cloud also made a circle. Some of the People bent over to look at bones in the grass, then others followed them. The People could find only one hole in the skull not two holes. What Bad One made just one hole? The People made their eyes small and their faces look as when they try to find People coming back to the cave and tree-homes. Then they sniffed the air and made their ears move one way and another. Did the hole-maker even have a smell?

Suddenly the People stopped moving. They felt that something was hiding in the grass a few jumps away. The People took small steps backwards towards the water and then stopped again. They heard a sound coming from the grass, but not a growl or a hiss. It was a *hooosa* sound like the People make. They moved towards the sound. Then the young one called Good-Follower ran into the grass towards the sound. Then he came back pulling two young ones with him. The bigger one could make more People. The two began to moan and cry when they saw all the strange faces looking at them.

Blowing-Ground got on her hands and knees and looked into the eyes of the young ones and grinned. The People backed away from the young ones but kept looking at them. Black-Cloud came up to them with water in her hands and said *eewoo*. The two jumped towards her and licked the water from her hands.

The sky was getting dark and it was time to hide. The People began to walk back up the hill to the nearest tree-homes. Good-Follower pushed the two young ones to follow the People but they stood still. As Blowing-Ground and Black-Cloud began to walk away they turned and held out their hands to the two young ones. The young ones reached out and grabbed hands and walked with the People.

Once in the tree-homes the People did not sleep but saw behind their eyes the ones with no names. The *huh* look was on every branch. Where did these young ones come from? Why did they look like the People? What sounds make their names? The long walk to the water did not make the *woo-ong* feelings of the People go away but made the feelings crawl on their skins like little black things. So many new things were coming to the People.

36. Hear My Tale of Two Names

The sky went from black to grey to yellow and the sky-dwellers made sounds in the tree-homes and some Bad Ones howled. The People were also a long walk away from their cave.

Sign-Reader was watching the light circle come back into the sky and waiting for the People to leave the tree-homes. She could see behind her eyes the way home. She looked to see if the young ones with no name were going to follow the People and saw that they were. Now the two were not afraid of the People and gripped whatever arm or hand was nearest. They looked up at the new faces around them with wide white eyes. Sign-Reader began walking towards where the light circle looked into the eyes of the People.

The People made noise as they walked among the tree-homes and within the tall grass. They hooted and hissed and whooped and howled and made the *hooo* sound with their chins sticking out and their lips making a small circle. The new young ones made the same sounds as they jumped and hopped. The People looked and them and grinned. They could not see behind their eyes where the young ones came from or why the young ones looked like them but still the People were happy and not afraid. But they would be happier once back at their cave and tree-homes.

The light in the sky was near the ground when the People began to smell their home. They walked faster with some walking past Sign-Reader, who walked slowly to look back at the People following her. The People were happy to be back and they hugged and kissed each other and hummed and purred soft sounds. As they hugged and kissed they sniffed each other and saw behind their eyes the People as more than the People.

But they did not smell themselves on the young ones found at the water. The People looked at them with a *huh* face and some of the People did not kiss them or hug them as they did the others whose scent they had smelled many times. The young ones tried to hug and kiss the others but they could not make the sounds the People made and they could not make the *huh* face.

The People inside the cave sat on the ground with their legs crossed and their eyes looking at the new young ones. The young ones kept turning their heads to look into the eyes of the People, and made them grin by making strange sounds, but the People looked at each other without grinning.

Suddenly Never-See-Me reached out and made her finger look at the one who could make more people. She made the sound for *Bright-Water*. She made the sound again and again as she made her finger jump back and forth in the air. The young one then made the same sound. Never-See-Me then looked at the other young one and made the sound *Strong-Clinger*. Her finger went back and forth as she made the sound again and again. Now Bright-Water put her hand on the other one and she said softly into his ear the sound *Strong-Clinger*. He looked up at her and made the same sound. The People grinned and hooted and touched each other.

Now that the People had found out their names, Bright-Water and Strong-Clinger began to smell like the People.

37. Hear My Tale about Eating the Sun

It was lighttime but the People were in the cave because the cave was cool and had water and the Bad Ones did not want to come there. The People were lying on the ground or sitting with their backs against the walls. They picked crawling things off each other and the young ones pushed small stones back and forth. Those outside the cave felt the wind on their skin.

Burning-Stick was outside on the ground among the tree-homes looking for logs to burn when no heat came came from the sky. The only sounds were the soft humming of the People and the buzzing of small little things moving through the air.

The brightness of the sky circle made the People outside the cave shut their eyes and look down at the ground where they sat with their legs folded under them. Their eyes were so small and tight that they could not see even the many small black things crawling on the ground. Sometimes the heads of the People would start to move slowly forward to the ground but then jump back up. The People did not fear anything and were happy.

But Burning-Stick kept his eyes open as he moved under the branches of the tree-homes looking for logs. His nose did not smell any Bad Ones because Bad Ones did not chase anything when the air was as hot as burning logs. Burning-Stick picked up many logs and held them across both arms. When a stick fell back to the ground he would pick it up again. He used the bottom of his jaw to keep them from falling.

Then a log fell from his arms and Burning-Stick could not see it. It was his foot that found it. But then he could not see his foot. He looked up and found that there were many things he could not see. *Huh?* Darkness was coming in the lighttime. He looked up into the sky where the circle of light and heat was going away. He let out the sound *woo-ong? woo-ong?*

The People outside the cave opened their eyes and looked down at him. Then they turned their heads to look where he was looking in the sky. Their eyes did not tighten because nighttime was coming during the lighttime. This was a new thing the People had not seen before. they began to make the sound of fear--*eevooorr*.

The People inside the cave heard the sound and some went further back into the cave where the water lived. But the small ones Good-Crawler and Good-Follower ran to the opening of the cave followed by Strong-Branches and No-Hair. They looked up where they saw the others looking to find that the circle of light was almost gone. The world was dark but not as dark as when the night comes. Good-Crawler shouted *ishsee!* He turned to look at the others around him and they too said *ishsee*. Still a w*oo-ong* look was also on their faces.

The circle of light always found a place to hide from the Bad Ones just as the People always found a place to hide. But now the Bad Ones had found the light circle before it could hide in the ground and they were eating it bit by bit.

The People saw behind their eyes no more light or heat coming from the sky. They saw only nighttime, with Bad Ones always wanting to eat. A feeling of *ehe ehe* gripped the People outside the cave and they shivered in the heat of the day. If the People always had to hide in the cave or tree-homes, how would they eat? How would they drink? These were the things that the People saw behind their eyes as they looked up into the dark sky where the circle of light and heat was being eaten before it could hide in the ground.

The People who saw this thing ran back into the cave where the others were hiding. They pressed together and hugged each other and tried to stop shaking from the cold that was now inside them. The People who did not leave the cave made the sound *woo-ong*? The others pointed up and made a circle with their hands and said *ishsee! ishsee!* This made those who stayed inside the cave have the *????* face. They shared the fear but had not seen what those outside the cave had seen.

Then all those inside the cave heard the sound *heeheeah!* The call came from Burning-Stick who had stayed outside to watch the Bad Ones eat the circle. *Heeheeah! Heeheeah!* The People were afraid to leave the cave but they wanted to see why Burning-Stick was not afraid. The People moved slowly to the opening of the cave and went from darkness to light. They looked up into the sky and had to make their eyes small and tight again.

Above their heads was a new circle of light and heat. The old one had been eaten but a new one followed it and had not been eaten. The People looked at this new circle and shouted up at it *ishsee! Ishsee! Ishsee!* They did not want this new one to be eaten as the old one had been eaten. They stayed outside the cave to see if the new circle would find a place to hide before the Bad Ones came back again. When Burning-Stick saw the new circle in the sky, he bent over to pick up the many logs he dropped. The People were happy that there would be heat and light inside the cave and outside the cave.

38. Hear My Tale of a Grass-Eater in a Tree-Home

The People were hungry for meat, especially the young ones. It was time to look for red bones left in the grass by the Bad Ones. But the young ones were not ready to run from the Bad Ones so some of the People had to stay with them in the cave and tree-homes.

But the People who stayed behind were afraid that they would not get any meat. The People looked into each other's eyes to find out what to do.

Eyes-that-Laugh pointed to Blowing-Ground, No-Hair, Never-See-Me, Cave-Finder, Tall-as-Grass, Burning-Stick and Far-Cloud. They should look for meat and what they brought back for their own young ones they should share with the People who stayed behind. The People nodded. So most of the People stayed and some went into the tall grasses to pick meat from bones.

The People did not like to walk through the tall grasses because the Bad Ones that hid there were hard to see. The Bad Ones were easy to smell but maybe the People were easy to smell too. The People walked slowly and stopped often to lift their noses and sniff. The People were most afraid of the Bad Ones with yellow and black hair around their heads because they had big mouths and long teeth. Despite their fear, the People followed the Bad Ones because they left the most food and they could not break open skulls. But the People could break open them open and eat the meat inside. Looking for meat always made the People happy and afraid at the same time.

Eyes-that-Laugh, Blowing-Ground, No-Hair, Never-See-Me, Cave-Finder, Tall-as-Grass, Burning-Stick and Far-Cloud walked slowly through grass they could not see over, so they were always sniffing sniffing sniffing.

Yet, they did not sniff the grass-eater that ran past them as if chased by flames. The grass-eater jumped over a log and hit the branch of a tree-home and fell to the ground with a squeal. It was only then that they saw the Bad One that was chasing it jump on it and bite into its neck until the legs of the grass-eater stopped kicking. The People did not move. They were afraid that the Bad One would smell their fear. This Bad One could climb tree-homes.

The Bad One was too busy lifting the grass-eater from the ground to smell the People. It put two of its legs on one side of the grass-eater and two on the other side and then began climbing the tree-home. It found a big branch and put the grass-eater over it so that its head and front legs were on one side and its two back legs on the other. This is not the way the People put themselves on branches. Then the Bad One began to eat. The smells of thick red water and meat filled the air and made the mouths of the People wet. They could see meat falling to the ground from the mouth of the Bad One. It did not look at the falling meat. The People wanted to run and grab it off the ground but they were too afraid to move or make a sound because they saw behind their eyes the mouth and tongue and teeth of the Bad One biting into them.

The Bad One made eating sounds as it pushed its face into the insides of the grass-eater between the back legs where the meat was softest. When the Bad One raised its head to look around, the People could see that its mouth was covered with red and bits of white. The long tongue of the Bad One came out and licked in a circle. Then the Bad One began to bite again and again at one of the back legs of the grass-eater. It bit and pulled as it held the grass-eater on the branch. It finally pulled the back leg free and held it in its mouth. It then walked head first down the tree-home to the ground. The Bad One went into the grass pushing it down with the leg in its mouth. The grass-eater was left hanging like food that grows from branches.

The People looked into each other's eyes. What to do? Blowing-Ground showed them. He ran to grab some meat on the ground and Far-Cloud followed. But there was more meat left. Cave-Finder ran and grabbed it and came back to the People hiding in the grass. There was no tree-home to climb to see if the Bad One was coming back but the People sniffed and sniffed the air.

No-Hair then ran to the tree and climbed to where the grass-eater was hanging with its head and two legs on one side of a branch and its one back leg on the other. Red water was hanging down from the legs but now it did not drip to the ground.

No-Hair pushed her hands inside the warm body and grabbed as much meat as she could hold. Down she came and she ran back to the People.

Tall-as-Grass did the same thing but he could not come down from the branch as she had done because the Bad One had come back and saw Tall-as-Grass up in the tree-home. The People shrieked and yelled *ishsee*! The Bad One did not hear the People but looked only at Tall-as-Grass. Pushing its back down, the Bad One made a great jump from the ground into the branch, but Tall-as-Grass was already climbing higher. His hands left red sign on the branches. The higher he climbed the higher climbed the Bad One.

Burning-Stick saw the Bad One high in the tree looking up at Tall-as-Grass. He ran to the tree-home and jumped up and grabbed the back leg of the grass-eater. He pulled and pulled and then hung from the back leg and made his feet go in a circle. The leg moved but did not fall down. Then Never-See-Me ran to him and also hung from the back leg and they both made their feet go in a circle. The leg made the sound that sticks make when the People step on them and it fell to the ground. Never-See-Me and Burning-Stick picked it up in their arms and ran back to where the People were hiding in the grass.

The Bad One heard the noise of the leg breaking and falling to the ground, and it turned its head to look down. All it saw was the leg of the grass-eater running away into the grass. It growled and slid down the tree-home and began running at the People even before its back feet were on the ground. The People were afraid but they did not drop the meat and they did not run away.

They did something new and they did it without looking into each other's eyes. They pushed against each other and jumped out of the grass with their wet red hands high above their heads and they screamed *ahhhhhggggggg* so loud that the Bad One stopped as if it had run into a rock.

Never before had the Bad One something with many screaming heads and even more red hands. While the Bad One was still looking at this new thing Tall-as-Grass dropped from branch to branch and landed on the ground without a sound. He ran into the grass and made a big circle to get back to the People. The Bad One blinked and turned and ran back to the tree-home. It jumped up and grabbed a front leg and pulled the grass-eater to the ground. Holding what was left of the grass-eater in its mouth the Bad One ran back to where its new ones were waiting for food. The Bad One was happy it was left with this much meat.

The People walked back to the cave with enough meat for everyone. On the way they began to see again behind their eyes the new thing they had done to make a Bad One afraid of them.

39. Hear My Tale of a Trap

While looking for the small soft red things that hide in bushes, the People heard squeals and snorts. They looked into each other's eyes to sense what the People should do. Should they run back to the cave and the tree-homes or follow Sign-Reader towards the noises that pulled on their ears? The People were afraid but their ears and eyes and Sign-Reader made them walk slowly towards the bellows and snorts. The sound did not come from Bad Ones but grass-eaters. The People were afraid of grass-eaters because the bones on their heads and their hard and sharp feet sometimes hurt the People. But sometimes the People had to see what made them afraid.

As the People followed Sign-Reader the noises became louder. The feet of the People began to move more quickly as did the feet in their chests. Sign-Reader and First-to-Shout were the first to see what was making the noises of fear and pain, and they held out their arms to stop the People from going too far. A grass-eater as big and as black as a rock was trying to get its legs out of deep mud. This grass-eater had huge bones coming out of its head that went out and then came back like arms trying to hug. The head of the grass-eater went back and forth and spit thick water from its mouth. It was making the noises that put fear into the People.

The People were afraid that the noises would bring the Bad Ones but they did not want to go back to the cave and the tree-homes because the grass-eater was meat. Meat for everyone for a long time. The People looked into each other's eyes for a sign of what to do. The grass-eater might run away. Or the Bad Ones might come to eat it and maybe the People too. Then Bright-Water picked up a rock and tossed it at the head of the grass-eater. The others then picked up rocks and began throwing them at the grass-eater too.

'It bellowed and jerked and tried to jump but it couldn't move away from the rocks thrown by the People. Then Strong-Clinger picked up a sharp stick and ran up to the grass-eater and pushed the stick into the meat hanging between the front and back legs. The grass-eater squealed and tried to hug Strong-Clinger with the bones on its head but it could not reach him. Then others grabbed sticks and went back and forth sticking them into the grass-eater. Some sticks made holes where thick red water came out and dropped on the ground. Soon the legs of the grass-eater broke like sticks and its head fell forward and its body fell on the mud.

The People stared at what they had done. 'Now what?' their faces seemed to say.

They tried biting through the skin but their teeth were not long and sharp like the teeth of the Bad Ones. They tried breaking through the skin with their fingers but they did not have the long and sharp fingers of the Bad Ones. Some of them pushed their hands into the holes made by the sticks but they could not pull out any meat this way. Night-Sky-Mover pulled out the tongue but this was not enough meat for all the People.

Then Strong-Clinger picked up a flat stone as big as his hand and went to the back end of the grass-eater and used the stone to bite through the thick skin until there was red meat. The rest of the People began looking for stones to do the same thing. They stabbed and cut and pulled as fast as they could. They ate as they worked because they also wanted to take as much meat back to the cave and the tree-homes as they could carry. Their bodies were covered in thick red water and the smell of it filled the air. The big sky-dwellers already were making circles in the air and soon the Bad Ones would smell the meat and they too would be coming to eat.

The first Bad Ones to come were the ones with thick necks and rounded ears. They never came alone. These Bad Ones could break bones with their mouths. They hooted and squealed all the time. The People were afraid of them but this time they wanted to keep the meat they had made. Never-See-Me and Far-Cloud and even Quiet One made the Bad Ones wait by throwing stones and sticks at them and howling and screaming and jumping and spinning and running back and forth.

The Bad Ones stopped hooting and just looked at the People and then walked backwards. The People stood up and howled and swung their arms. The Bad Ones turned and went backwards into the darkness of the tree-homes looking at the People and not where their feet were taking them. The People kept their meat this time but it would not be as easy when more and bigger Bad Ones came for it.

The hands of the People moved as if blown by a strong wind. They cut and pulled and twisted whatever meat they could carry back to the caves and the tree-homes, and they covered themselves with meat until the hair on their bodies was hidden and they were dripping with dark red water. Some of them put meat on sharp sticks or put it over logs as if the meat was sleeping in a tree-home.

When their ears heard the first roars of the yellow Bad Ones, the People followed Sign-Reader home. The People felt powerful because now the People were leaving meat for the Bad Ones.

40. Hear My Tale about the Return of Fast-Climber

One lighttime the People were lying on the rocks taking pleasure in the heat from the circle in the sky and the footsteps inside them were slow and soft. They could not smell or see any Bad Ones and they felt no fear. Behind their eyes they saw the soft food on tree-homes. Then their ears heard noises in the tall grass.

The People were not afraid because Bad Ones did not make such a noise. But something was. Soon all the People were standing up and big-eyeing where the grass was moving. They could see someone with a head and arms and legs. The person was coming towards them but moving one way and then another like a sky-dweller or stinger as it came closer. The People looked and waited and made the sound *woo-ong?* The footsteps inside their chests were moving faster now.

Out of the grass came Fast-Climber. The People did not like this. They could close their eyes and see the bad things he had done. But this was not the same Fast-Climber.

His eyes moved as if he were trying to follow the sky-dwellers as they went one way and another through the air. His head moved back and forth and side to side but he was not making signs to others. His mouth made many soft sounds that meant nothing to the ears of the People. He moved from one leg to another without walking. He did not always see the People or hear them. When he got to open ground he stood on one foot and then dragged the other foot to make a circle around him. His hands moved in and out and his fingers opened and closed. The People watched Fast-Climber but kept away from him.

The People looked into each other's eyes and made the "?" face. The People were not afraid of Fast-Climber because now he did not pull or push any of the People or try to hit them with his hands. He did not swing sticks or toss logs at them. But what should the People do with him? This was new for the People. Finally Strong-Branches went to Fast-Climber and hugged him. Fast-Climber did not move away.

After a time he stopped moving from one leg to another and his hands and arms stopped moving in and out and up and down. Instead of letting his head fall to one side Fast-Climber laid it next to Strong-Branches' head. The People saw this and moved to where the two stood. They kept making the sound *woo-ong?* but they reached out to touch Fast-Climber as the arms of Strong-Branches made a circle around him. Fast-Climber stopped making soft noises to himself.

The People then slowly moved towards the cave and Fast-Climber had to move with them. Inside the dark cave he did not jump or move but lay down on the ground and closed his eyes. But even when his eyes were closed they made little circles and tried to open.

When the circle of light opened the eyes of the People it did not open the eyes of Fast-Climber. No-Hair went to him and pushed open the eyes of Fast-Climber but his eyes did not look at No-Hair but looked at the top of the cave but did not see it. They saw something far away as if the top of the cave was not there. No-Hair and Cave-Finder lifted Fast-Climber and made him stand on his feet. They then took him outside the cave into the light. Fast-Climber began to move back and forth and swing his arms and hands one way and another as if he were falling to the ground and was trying to grab branches as he fell through them. The People had to find food but they did not want to leave Fast-Climber alone. The Bad Ones might find him and Fast-Climber could no longer climb fast.

So Sign-Reader and Water-Jumper took Fast-Climber by the arms and made him walk with the People. But he did not walk like the People. He jumped from one foot to another and turned in circles and sometimes fell to the ground and pushed his face into the dirt or grabbed dirt in his hands and tossed the dirt on the back of his head. But he did not try to leave the People. The People looked at Fast-Climber and their faces made the sign "?".

The People finally found tree-homes with much food hanging from them. The food was red, yellow, and green. They reached up or climbed up and grabbed the food and put them in their mouths. They pressed the food against their teeth to fill their mouths with water. Sometimes they moved their teeth side to side and back and forth to eat the skins and what they could not eat they spit on the ground. They grunted with pleasure.

But Fast-Climber did not grab the food hanging from the branches. Instead he grabbed the branches and hung there like the food. His legs went over the branch and his hands reached for the ground. He swung back and forth and hooted with pleasure. The People looked at him and clicked their teeth and hooted along with Fast-Climber.

When Fast-Climber dropped to the ground the People held him down and pushed the soft food into his mouth and water ran down both sides of his face. Fast-Climber ate most of the food but the parts too hard to chew he spit up into the air as high as he could and hooted through his teeth as the food fell back down on his face and the heads of the People holding him. This made the People hoot louder and their loud hoots made the sky-dwellers jump up from the tree-homes and hide themselves in the sky.

What Fast-Climber was doing gave the People much pleasure. Now the People were happy that he had come back to them, even if he had not brought Water-Fall with him.

41. Hear My Tale about Fast-Climber and a Bad One

The People liked to watch Fast-Climber because he made them hoot and click their teeth and slap their hands from pleasure. They often sat on the ground beneath the rocks of the cave when the light circle was in the sky to watch Fast-Climber eat ground-runners and crawlers. He would lie on the ground and let the crawlers cover his body and hands and then he would lick them off his fingers and put his hands back on his body to get more to eat. Sometimes he would take a stick and put it into the ground where the crawlers lived and then take it out and pull it over his tongue to lick off the things crawling on the stick. Sometimes he would make water into the holes where the ground-runners hid and then catch and eat them when they came out. The eyes of Fast-Climber now could see things.

It came to pass that during one lighttime the People were watching Fast-Climber fall on the ground and then get up and jump and then fall on the ground and then make his body go in circles and do other things that made the People laugh. Suddenly Blowing-Ground watching near the cave yelled *ishsee evooorr!* The little ones were grabbed up and the People on the ground ran to tree-homes or to the rocks near the cave. The open ground was empty. Except for Fast-Climber.

From the tree-homes and rocks the People could see Fast-Climber still making
Making circles with his feet in the dirt and falling down and moving his body one way and another. Had he not heard the warning sound? Why did he not run and hide? W*oo-ong?* Then the eyes of the People moved from Fast-Climber to the edge of the grass, where they saw a Bad One with teeth so long that they could not fit into its mouth. It moved slowly from the grass into the opening, its eyes looking at Fast-Climber and nothing else.

The Bad One made the sound the sky makes when it became black and threw light into the ground. Then it made its back go lower as the People do when they jump. Why did Fast-Climber not run away and hide? The People's faces said "?"

Fast-Climber looked at the Bad One and began to hoot the same way he hooted when he hung by his legs from the branches in the tree-home. He jumped from one leg to the other and then he jumped up and down as he turned in a circle. The Bad One stood up and looked closely at Fast-Climber and only at Fast-Climber. Then Fast-Climber walked towards the Bad One still hooting and now making his arms and hands look like branches in the wind.

The Bad One pulled back its head and kept looking. Then Fast-Climber stopped, lowered his head and jumped, swinging his feet into the air and over his head back onto the ground in a big circle. His hands did not touch the ground. When his feet came back to the ground Fast-Climber was again looking into the eyes of the Bad One, which now opened and closed very fast. The People made the sound *haaahhhh*. Without a sound the Bad One jumped backwards, turned and ran into the grass.

The People saw what had happened. How did Fast-Climber make the Bad One afraid of him? The People looked and made the sound *woo-ong?* again and again but they also hooted and clicked their teeth. When Fast-Climber came back to the cave, the People gave Fast-Climber much to eat and Black-Cloud and Night-Sky-Mover gave him a place to rest.

Fast-Climber had given gave the People much pleasure but now he also gave them much strength. The People saw many times behind their eyes what Fast-Climber did to make the Bad One run away.

42. Hear My Tale about a Re-Telling

When the People saw things behind their eyes, they often saw the same things and sometimes at the same time. What gave them pleasure was to see when the People were strong and not afraid. They often saw Eyes-that-Laugh make the Bad One go back into the grass. Or Strong-Branches make the stingers bite the tree climber. Or Hair-on-Face being pulled out of the mouth of the Old One in the river. Or Fast-Climber making the Bad One with long teeth run away. Seeing these things again and again behind their eyes made the People happy and strong.

Looking at burning logs often gave the People pictures of things that had happened. One night the People were sitting in the cave looking at the burning logs and at the little lights that climbed to the top of the cave. The footsteps inside their chests were slow and soft. The People listened to the breaking sounds made by the burning logs. Suddenly Fast-Climber stood up and ran in a circle in front of the People bending over to look into their eyes. This too gave the People pleasure. They liked to watch the many things that Fast-Climber did. As he ran in a circle the People hooted softly and clicked their teeth in pleasure.

As suddenly as he started Fast-Climber stopped and fell on his hands and knees. He did not look at anyone but at something inside the cave no one else could see. Then he made his back come up and his backside go down as if he were getting ready to jump forward as the Bad Ones did when they take their food. He growled. The People stopped clicking their teeth and looked at what Fast-Climber was doing. He growled again and opened his mouth as wide as he could and moved his head to show his teeth to the People. A few of the People near him moved away, afraid that Fast-Climber might try to hurt them again.

Then Fast-Climber stood up and turned and looked at the spot where he was just on his hands and knees growling. He turned in circles and moved his hands and arms and jumped to make his feet go in a circle over his head just as he had done in the open ground in front of the Bad One with long teeth. The People watched everything he did and did not take their eyes off him. Then Fast-Climber fell back down on his hands and knees and turned and pushed through the People who were sitting at the opening of the cave. They turned their heads to see where Fast-Climber was going, and how far. Once outside the circle, Fast-Climber stood up and turned to the People and clicked his teeth and spread his lips wide to make the sign of happiness and pleasure.

By the light of the burning logs the People saw again what Fast-Climber had done to make the Bad One afraid of him. They saw it both with their eyes and behind their eyes. But there was no Bad One to see. There was only Fast-Climber. Bad One. Fast-Climber. Bad One. Fast-Climber. *Huh* said the faces of the People.

The new thing that Fast-Climber had done gave the People great joy. Only a few were made afraid by what they saw. The others stood up and hooted and moved from one foot to the other and made smacking sounds with their lips. They went over to Fast-Climber and touched him on his head and back. After his return to the People, Fast-Climber was making them see many new things behind their eyes. And now with their eyes.

43. Hear My Tale about a Re-Re-Telling!

What Fast-Climber had done the night when he was both the Bad One and Fast-Climber was often seen by the People behind their eyes. But the People wanted to see it again with open eyes. They would often go to Fast-Climber and make him go down on his hands and knees and then they would look at him and wait for him to growl and do all the other things he did that night. But they had to wait night after night for Fast-Climber to do this because he was seeing other things behind his eyes. When the People came to make him become the Bad One Fast-Climber would stand up and turn in circles and hoot or spit water. This was what made Fast-Climber happy.

It happened that one night the People again were trying to make Fast-Climber crawl on his hands and knees and growl like the Bad One with long teeth. But again Fast-Climber jumped up and began to hoot and kick his legs one way and another as he often did when he did not want to be the Bad One and then be Fast-Climber and then Bad One and then Fast-Climber. He shook his head and made the sound *noooah*.

Burning-Stick watched this night after night. Then behind his eyes he also saw something new. He stood up suddenly and left the circle of People and fell on his hands and knees in front of Fast-Climber. The People looked at Burning-Stick and did not move. Burning-Stick looked up as

Fast-Climber and opened his mouth to show his teeth and then made a *grrrRRRRRRR* sound. The sound made even the flames of the burning logs move away in fear.

Fast-Climber looked at Burning-Stick with the big white eyes a person has when about to step on a Bad One lying in the grass. Without taking his eyes off Burning-Stick, Fast-Climber hooted and jumped as he had done in the open ground in front of the Bad One. Burning-Stick then drew back his head as the Bad One had done. The two of them were making the sounds and movements the People wanted to see again, and their eyes also became big by seeing it again.

Burning-Stick made his back go up and his backside go down as the Bad One had done. Suddenly Fast-Climber could see behind his eyes what he should do next. He made his arms and hands go one way and another and then lowered his body and jumped up and made his head go down and his feet make a circle over his head and land on the ground without his hand touching anything. This made Burning-Stick do as the Bad One had done. He jumped back and ran out of the cave on his hands and knees.

The People hooted and jumped and patted both Burning-Stick and Fast-Climber on their heads and backs. Eyes-that-Laugh pushed through the others to hug and kiss Burning-Stick. The growl of Burning-Stick was better than the growl of Fast-Climber. It made the People feel that the Bad One was there when it was not there. This new thing that Fast-Climber and Burning-Stick had done made the People feel strong and gave them more pleasure than the first new thing. The People often saw behind their eyes what Fast-Climber and Burning-Stick had done. When they looked at Burning-Stick and Fast-Climber they pulled back their lips and made *ha ha ha* sound.

To give pleasure to the People, Burning-Stick and Fast-Climber often made their growls and jumps when the logs were burning, and many of the People who once spent the night in the tree-homes now spent the night in the cave where new things happened around the burning logs.

44. Hear My Tale about the New Thing with Long Teeth

It happened that one lighttime Burning-Stick walked away from the People into the tall grass. People did not go into the tall grass alone because it was good to have more than one nose to smell the Bad Ones hiding there. The circle in the sky was becoming red when Burning-Stick came back out of the tall grass. He carried with him the white skull of a Bad One. It was not easy to find a skull with so many sharp teeth. Sharp teeth made the People afraid and they did not pick up these skulls and carry them around as Burning-Stick was now doing. The faces of the People made the sign ???? as they watched Burning-Stick carry the head bone of the Bad One into the cave.

Soon the People heard again and again the same noise they heard when they kicked a head bone with their feet. Was Burning-Stick kicking the skull with his feet? Suddenly the skull came rolling out of the cave, and Burning-Stick came after it and picked it up and tossed it back with both hands as hard as he could off the side of the cave. Was Burning-Stick angry at the head bone? Then he and the skull were lost in the darkness. The noise of bone kicking began again. The People looked into each other's eyes but could find nothing to give them a picture of what Burning-Stick was doing. The noises stopped only when Burning-Stick came out of the cave without the skull to join the People sitting around the burning logs.

The sky was dark but the burning logs made the light come back to the cave. The People wanted to see Burning-Stick and Fast-Climber growl and jump again. It always began with some of the People holding on to Fast-Climber and leading him to the opening of the cave and then looking at Burning-Stick. The others would then sit around the flames so they could see what the two of them would do. Some of the People would begin hooting to make Burning-Stick or Fast-Climber do something. The bodies of the People moved as if crawlers were in their hair.

Fast-Climber stood where he had stood so often before and Burning-Stick got on his hands and knees as he had done so often. It was always Burning-Stick who began by growling and then opening his mouth to show his teeth as he always did. But this time when he opened his mouth, two long sharp teeth were pointing at Fast-Climber and at the

People. Under his lips Burning-Stick had placed the long teeth from the skull of the Bad One. Fast-Climber shrieked and jumped back into the burning logs, which broke into many small flames and jumping lights. The People hooted and growled and fell back to the walls of the cave. Those who could see the sharp teeth coming out of the mouth of Burning-Stick yelled *eevooorr!* Burning-Stick stayed on his hands and knees and turned his head one way and the other so all the People could see why Fast-Climber and the others were afraid of him.

No one moved until Fast-Climber walked towards Burning-Stick and gave out the cry of *aya aya!* Then he made the *ha ha ha* sound and turned his head back and forth to look at the People. Fast-Climber was no longer afraid but pleased at what Burning-Stick had done. The People came out of hiding from behind each other and watched as Fast-Climber stood in front of Burning-Stick and made his arms move and his body jump. Burning-Stick made his backside go down and growled his loud growl. And pointed his sharp teeth at Fast-Climber as if to bite him.

This nighttime Fast-Climber bent down lower and jumped higher than he had ever done, even on that day when he was looking at the Bad One itself. When Fast-Climber made his jump, Burning-Stick did as he always did and crawled into the darkness just outside the cave. The People hooted and screamed and made new sounds not heard before to show their pleasure with this new thing that Burning-Stick had done. It made the Bad One more there than not there. The People hugged Burning-Stick and Fast-Climber and each other from the joy they felt in this new thing. What Fast-Climber and Burning-Stick were doing the People began to call *eeooree*.

45. Hear My Tale of a New Ecooree

Now when the nighttime came, the People no longer felt fear but something else. They felt as if they had little black things crawling everywhere inside them. Each night the People waited to see if Burning-Stick and Fast-Climber would make a new thing by the light of the burning logs.

It happened that one night some of the People were again walking towards Fast-Climber to help him stand in front of Burning-Stick so that the two could growl and jump as the People wanted them to. But something new happened. Eyes-that-Laugh moved between the People and Fast-Climber and said softly *noooah noooah noooah*. As she said this she turned her head to look at all the People with happy eyes. She held out her arms and made a space in the cave between her and the People. The People moved back and most sat down to see what new thing would happen next.

Then from out of the darkness of the cave came a roar like the roar made by the Bad One with yellow skin. The sound was so loud that some of the People hid behind others and they all turned around to look where the roar had come from inside the darkness of the cave. Another roar. The eyes of the People did not blink. Then the People heard grunts and coughs.

Out of the darkness crawled Blowing-Ground on her hands and knees. This was new. Blowing-Ground had not made the sound of the Bad One before and Fast-Climber and

Burning-Stick did not come out of the cave. As Burning-Stick had done, Blowing-Ground had placed under her lips two long sharp teeth taken from the skull of the Bad One. But Blowing-Ground did another new thing. Around her neck was a woven circle of long grass which stuck out and touched the dirt. The grass was as yellow as the yellow hair around the faces of the Bad Ones that ate but were not eaten.

Blowing-Ground crawled to the edge of the yellow and red light from the burning logs and lay flat on the ground with her eyes closed and without making another sound. Now Eyes-that-Laugh ran towards Blowing-Ground and Blowing-Ground rose up with a growl. Eyes-that-Laugh stopped and stood without moving. She looked at Blowing-Ground and Blowing-Ground looked back at her and neither moved. The People saw behind their eyes the time this had happened near the bones with meat. They saw again Eyes-that-Laugh running to the bones and the Bad One suddenly rising from the grass to keep the meat. They saw again behind their eyes the way Eyes-that-Laugh had looked into the eyes of the Bad One and made it afraid of her.

Blowing-Ground turned away and went to hide in the darkness of the cave as the Bad One had turned away to hide in the grass. When Blowing-Ground could not be seen, Eyes-that-Laugh turned around and looked at the People who were watching from behind her. She pulled back her lips and made the sound *hah hah hah hah*.

The People hooted and *hah*-ed back to her and hugged each other and patted Eyes-that-Laugh and Blowing-Ground for the new things they had done. Here was another *eeooree* that made them feel happy and strong. What other new things that gave the People pleasure would be done by the light of the burning logs? And who would do them?

46. Hear My Tale about a Watcher

They People no longer feared the night but now wanted it to come. Their eyes no longer searched the darkness for Bad Ones and their ears no longer heard the screams of the night. Their eyes and ears now stayed inside the cave to see and hear the *eeooree* which made them happy and strong. But the People inside the cave were now so much inside the cave that they did not feel they were being watched by others outside the cave.

Almost every night others were watching from the tree-home across the open ground as the People did things that the watchers had not seen before. *Huh? huh? huh?*. Watching the People in the cave was like watching the moving flames of burning logs. What had happened to the People? Had they eaten food that made them growl and jump and crawl? Had they become bad like the eaters of People with four legs?

This night the *eeooree* was about Strong-Branches saving the People by hitting the one with spots with the soft cave-home of the black-and-yellow stingers. To make this *eeooree*, Strong-Branches had found an empty stinger cave on the ground. The People looked inside to make sure. Night-Sky-Mover placed under her thin lips the long sharp teeth taken from the broken skull of a Bad One. This was not a new thing but Night-Sky-Mover did something else that was new. She had taken a blackened log from the flames and used it to make black spots on her body like the black spots on the body of the Bad One that climbs tree-homes.

There were no tree-homes inside the cave but there were rocks that tried to touch the top of the cave. Strong-Branches climbed up one of them and Night-Sky-Mover climbed up another. Night-Sky-Mover made her fingers curl and she swung her hands above her head as if she were trying to grab something above her. The rocks were close enough for Strong-Branches to hit Night-Sky-Mover with the empty stinger cave. When he did this, Night-Sky-Mover jumped to the ground and squealed and ran on her hands and feet into the darkness of the cave.

Strong-Branches looked at the People and pulled back his lips and make the *hah-hah* sound just as Eyes-that-Laugh had done. Another new thing had been done, and the People hooted and jumped and slapped their hands with pleasure, and their feet kicked the burning logs so that flames jumped up and put light into the trees outside the cave.

The eyes of Night-Sky-Mover, No-Hair, Cave-Finder and Sign-Reader followed the little lights as they rose into the night air. As they looked out across the open ground they saw something hiding in a tree-home. They ran outside the cave to see what was hiding from them but the little lights had gone into the black sky. But their ears heard the sounds of a small one and their noses smelled at least two people. By now others had come out of the cave to look at the things in the tree-home. Suddenly the sounds and smells went away and the People went back into the cave to see again behind their eyes Strong-Branches swinging his arm to hit the spotted Bad One with the home of the stingers. The People hooted and kicked again and patted Strong-Branches and Night-Sky-Mover for the *eeooree* that night.

Finally the People gathered in the cave and closed their eyes for the night. When the circle of light came back into the sky, Sign-Reader left the cave and walked slowly across the open ground with her back looking at the sky and her eyes almost touching the dirt. She walked around one of the tree-homes many times with her head bent so low her knees almost hit her chin. The People came out of the cave and watched what Sign-Reader was doing. Sign-Reader made sounds and movements that made the People see behind their eyes what she saw with her eyes.

She pointed to something on the ground at the bottom of the tree-home and bent over with her arms on her knees. She made the sound people make when making mud from their bottom. The People were pleased and said to Sign-Reader *hah hah hah hah*. But they also saw behind their eyes something that had watched them from the tree-home for a long time.

Sign-Reader put her eyes close to the tree-home and made the sign that there were two climbers, one small and one bigger. They went up together with the bigger one on the outside and the smaller one on the inside so it could not fall backwards to the ground.

The People made the sound *huh?* to each other as they walked about on the rocks of the cave. Sign-Reader looked up at the moving light in the sky and made the sign showing the circle going into the ground when the night came. She then made the sign for "hiding" and pointed a finger at Water-Jumper, Black-Cloud, and Burning-Stick. The People nodded. When the night came some of the People would not be in the cave watching the *eeooree* but they would be hiding in the darkness to see the people who were watching them from the tree-home. Sign-Reader made new things too.

47. Hear My Tale of Another Return

The circle of light once again found a place to hide, but the Bad One had already bitten it and made it red.

The People sat around the burning logs and their eyes opened and closed opened and closed as they watched the flames jump back and forth and up and down. They saw behind their eyes not only another *eeooree* but Sign-Reader, Water-Jumper, Black-Cloud, and Burning-Stick hiding outside the cave waiting to grab the others watching the People from the darkness of the tree-home.

This night Strong-Branches and Night-Sky-Mover again showed the People how the Bad One with spots was made to run away from the People before it ate them. As the People inside the cave hooted and jumped with pleasure, so did the People outside the cave waiting in the grass, who whooped and kicked and *hah-hah*-ed with the others.

The two hiding in the tree-home heard the noise beneath them and looked down to see People waiting in the grass to grab them. The two were afraid of the People because the People did many strange things. The two tried to get away by letting their bodies fall from branch to branch but they were not fast enough. When their feet touched the ground Sign-Reader, Water-Jumper, Black-Cloud, and Burning-Stick grabbed them and threw them to the ground and held them there. It was too dark for Sign-Reader and the others to see the faces of the watchers, so First-to-Shout slid down the rocks with a burning log and ran to where the People were holding down at the hiding ones.

The light from the burning log was put in front of the face of the bigger one and First-to-Shout, Sign-Reader, Water-Jumper, Black-Cloud, and Burning-Stick all went *haaaah!* They were again looking at the face of Water-Fall. Water-Fall had come back, and she brought with her a young one.

The People picked up Water-Fall and her young one and hugged them and kissed them and made soft sounds in their ears that said nothing but that were good to hear. Now Water-Fall was not afraid of the People. They were not sick from eating bad food and they had not become like the Bad Ones. They were not the same People she was taken from one night a long time ago.

Hugging her son, Water-Fall told the People that her child was named Long-Walker. Now Water-Fall and Long-Walker would not have to watch the *eeooree* from a tree-home but could watch it from inside the cave together with the People.

48. Hear My Tale of a Re-union

The People in the cave did what Sign-Reader, Water-Jumper, Black-Cloud, Burning-Stick and First-to-Shout had done when they saw the face of Water-Fall. They hugged and kissed her and they hugged and kissed her son Long-Walker too. The faces of many of the People said *huh?* but their faces also were happy that Water-Fall had returned to the People and brought another with her.

Standing in the cave, the People saw again behind their eyes many things about Water-Fall, Fast-Climber, and Water-Jumper. They saw again the time when Fast-Climber did things to make the People afraid of him. They saw again what they did to make him leave the cave and the tree-homes. They saw again the signs that showed that Water-Fall was dragged away from the People. They saw again Water-Jumper following the signs until he could not see them and the People had to go back before the Bad Ones came. They saw again Fast-Climber coming back to the People and doing new things that made them happy and not afraid. These sights jumped and skipped behind the eyes of the People until the People had to sit or else fall down. Seeing all these things made the faces of the People wrinkle into *huh?*

The People sat in a circle around the burning logs. They could not take their eyes away from Water-Fall and Long-Walker. Her return was like an *eeooree*. Then from the circle of unmoving eyes Fast-Climber rose up slowly. The

People now turned their eyes to him. What was Fast-Climber going to do? Was he going to jump and make his head go down and his feet go in a circle over his head and land on the ground? This would give pleasure to the People and to Water-Fall and Long-Walker too.

But Fast-Climber did not jump but walked slowly to Water-Fall and then fell on his knees. Just on his knees. He bent over and looked at the ground in front of her and did not move or make a sound. His hands were open and turned up as if asking for food.

Water-Fall looked at his bent head, and did not move at first or make a sound. But then she placed one hand softly on his head and made a sound only those next to her could hear—*aya, aya*. Water came from Fast-Climber's eyes. He stood up and went back to where he had been sitting. He did not look at the People but at the ground as if he were seeing behind his eyes the signs he left when he and the other took Water-Fall in the darkness long ago. Now the wrinkles were gone from the faces of the People.

Water-Fall looked over the People sitting in the red and yellow darkness of the flames and she stopped on the one she had often seen behind her own eyes. It was now Water-Fall who rose up slowly and walked to kneel in front of Water-Jumper. But she did not bow her head but looked into his eyes and uttered *eeookos*, the same sound the People made when eating the food that hangs on branches.

Water-Jumper bent over and pressed the front of his head against the front of her head and reached out and put his hands around her arms. He also said *eeookos*. Then he stood up and went into the cave where he lay down at night. He came out of the darkness of the cave with a yellow food that grows on tree-homes and went over to Long-Walker and gave it to him. Long-Walker pushed the food into his mouth and sucked his lips and squealed with pleasure. The People rocked back and forth and side to side and gave short hoots through their grinning mouths. Especially Fast-Climber.

49. Hear My Tale about the Young Ones Tale

When the hot light circle was high in the sky the young ones often sat on the ground below the cave and tossed bones in the air or at each other. They grinned and hooted as the bones went one way or another. The others sat on the rocks and picked crawling things out of their hair as they watched the young ones on the ground below them tossing bones.

Sometimes Fast-Climber sat on the ground and tossed bones with the young ones, or make them grin and hoot by jumping and swinging his arms and turning circles in the dirt. Fast-Climber made many noises as he jumped and hopped and turned. The young ones would watch him with big white eyes and they no longer saw the bones lying on the ground but only Fast-Climber doing the things that put fear into Bad Ones. Even Water-Fall would watch and hoot and grin. Sometimes the young ones would do what Fast-Climber did and make Fast-Climber grin and hoot too. The People did not feel afraid when Fast-Climber and the young ones did things that made the People grin and hoot.

At nighttime the People often wanted an *eeooree*. They would gather in a circle around the burning logs waiting for one of them to begin. Sometimes the People would wait for a long time, even until the next nighttime. Fast-Climber did not always want to be a Bad One. Strong-Branches did not always want to throw a soft cave home at Night-Sky-Mover. And sometimes the People wanted to see a new *eeooree* .

One nighttime the People were sitting in a circle waiting for one. They looked from side to side at each other but no one stood up or began to crawl and growl. Then Long-Walker rose up and looked into the eyes of Good-Crawler, Good-Follower, Quiet-One, Bright-Water and Strong-Clinger. They rose up too, and then they ran inside the cave. The People sitting in a circle around the burning logs had the *huh?* look on their faces.

Soon one of the young ones crawled out of the darkness of the cave into the moving colors of the burning logs. It was Long-Walker walking on his hands and his feet to make himself as big as he could. His body and head were covered by the yellow skin of a Bad One, under his lip were two long sharp bones, and his mouth was covered in red dirt as if he had been eating meat.

Long-Walker growled and turned his head one way and another and tried to bite the People closest to him, and the People yelled *eevooorr* and jumped away from him. Then out of the darkness of the cave came Good-Crawler, Good-Follower, Quiet-One, Bright-Water and Strong-Clinger. They had long sticks, stones, and a white skull with two long sharp bones coming out of it.

They quickly made a circle around Long-Walker and began to throw the stones at him and hit him with the sticks and jab him with sharp bones. As the People watched this new thing they also wanted to hit Long-Walker with sticks and stones. Long-Walker felt the stones and sticks and sharp bones and he did not want to be the Bad One anymore but he could not get through the circle of the young ones.

So Long-Walker stood up and pulled off the skin of the Bad One, took out the long bones under his lips and shouted *oooah!* The shout went into the cave and came back out again, and made the young ones stop throwing stones and hitting and jabbing him. Now the only sound in the cave was made by the burning logs.

The People stood still and behind their eyes they saw what had happened. They saw it and they saw it. Then they began to slowly grin and make low hoot sounds. The young ones joined in and the hoots became louder. Then Fast-Climber began to jump and hop and turn in circles. The power of *eeooree* always made the People feel strong, but this time it also made them feel fear.

Long-Walker did not grin and hoot as much as the others because more than any of the People, he felt the power of *eeooree*.

51. Hear My Tale about Leaving

The People had lived a long time in the same cave and tree-homes. The circle of light had come out of hiding many times to make the People warm and to show them where the Bad Ones were hiding and where food was waiting to be eaten.

But now the food was harder to find and water was no longer nearby. And now the cave and the tree-homes and the ground smelled of the People. The smell made some things stay away but other things come closer to find something to eat. The People wanted to eat new food and to see and smell new things. They looked into each other's eyes and saw that it was time to leave the cave and tree-homes and to find new ones somewhere else. But that somewhere they could not see behind their eyes.

Not all the People wanted to leave the cave and the tree-homes. Never-See-Me, Far-Cloud, Blowing-Ground, Good-Hider and others shook their heads and muttered *nooaah*. But Burning-Stick, Eyes-that-Laugh, Fast-Climber, First-to-Shout, Tall-as-Grass, Night-Sky-Mover, Sign-Reader and many others nodded and made the sounds *heeheeah* and *weeeahah*. The others still shook their heads and uttered the sound *nooaah*. The People would not be as many as they once were.

Soon the day came when many of the People walked away from the others. The first to walk away was Sign-Reader. Those wanting to leave the cave and the tree-homes followed her, and they were Bright-Water, Strong-Clinger, Long-Walker, Water-Jumper, Strong-Branches, Cave-Finder, No-Hair, Quiet-One, Black-Cloud, and others. Eyes-that-Laugh could not walk fast because she was going to have a new one. Burning-Stick walked next to her.

The People carried skulls filled with water and one grass-eater skull filled with hot burned logs, which they carried by putting a long bone through the eye holes. As they walked away they wanted to look back at Good-Hider, Never-See-Me, Far-Cloud, Blowing-Ground, and the others who stayed but they did not.

Instead they kept their eyes looking at the ground that was moving slowly under their feet. The People staying in the cave did not want to look at the People leaving the cave, and did not want to see the signs their feet left in the dirt as they walked away from them. No one hooted or shouted or clapped, but some made the sound *hooasa*.

Behind their eyes the People saw themselves coming together again. But in the darkness behind their eyes they could not see where or when that would be.

About The Author

Paul Trout (Ph D) is professor emeritus at Montana State University (Department of English). He has published widely in a number of areas, with his work appearing in professional journals as well as in *The Christian Science Monitor*, *The Washington Post*, *The Washington Times*, and *The Chronicle of Higher Education*. His work has been syndicated in periodicals in Germany, England, and Australia, and his essays on higher education have been anthologized in freshmen readers. When he stopped teaching Professor Trout began writing for his own satisfaction. That led to the publication of *Deadly Powers: Animal Predators and the Mythic Imagination*. Since then he has written *Imagining Phineas Gage: A Novel about the World's Most Famous Head Case* (in the hands of an agent), *Dawn Stories*, and *Atavistic Enchantments: Traces of the Paleolithic in Storytelling* (in revision). When he's not writing or reading, he enjoys watching movies and playing tennis, but not at the same time.

Made in the USA
Middletown, DE
17 May 2023

30765167R00111